MW00471798

I, AI

SCI-FI STORIES FOR THE TRANSHUMAN AGE

ANDRE K. GEORGE

Random Forest Press

BOULDER, COLORADO

Copyright © 2021 Andre K. George

All rights reserved.

The characters and events portrayed in this book are fictitious. Any
similarity to real persons, living or dead, is coincidental and not
intended by the author.

No part of this book may be reproduced, or stored in a retrieval system,
or transmitted in any form or by any means, electronic, mechanical,
photocopying, recording, or otherwise, without the written permission
of the author, Andre K. George.

ISBN-13: 978-1-956305-00-5

Cover design by Ravven at ravven.com

Library of Congress Cataloging-in-Publication Data is on file at the
Library of Congress, Washington, D.C.

Printed in the United States of America

Random Forest Press, Boulder, Colorado

Contents

To Angela and Anya, without whom I wouldn't have started
writing books.

The author wants to thank the following friends and colleagues for their encouragement and generous support of this book.

Rafael Gutierrez

Brett Karjalainen

Frank Murphy

Erik Salo

Ed Wiley

Preface

"The development of full artificial intelligence could spell the end of the human race....It would take off on its own, and re-design itself at an ever-increasing rate. Humans, who are limited by slow biological evolution, couldn't compete and would be superseded." — Stephen Hawking

The future is inevitable, unavoidable, and unstoppable as time itself.

Sometimes, it bursts through our doors, as loud and powerful as a freight train. On other occasions, it sneaks in almost undetected, invisible, quiet as a whisper. It is big on promises, rich in hopes and fears, and always full of surprises. Good and bad. The artificial intelligence (AI) revolution, which started in the 20th century, moves forward toward a destination that is still, generally, unknown to us. How far can it go? How far do we want it to go? Can we create a human-like AI? If so, can it be done without giving it human characteristics? Emotions? Humor? Fear? Anger? Envy? Loyalty? How will we interact with this human-like AI? Trust it? Use it? Fear it? Fight it?

How will it change the world that our great-great-grandchildren inherit from us? The world of transhumans, advanced humans who will be stronger, smarter, healthier, better-looking, and more talented than us. And, hopefully, not afraid of their artificial creations.

This collection of short sci-fi stories explores the future where humans and AI share not only the same space and time, but also jobs, needs, goals, and interests. A world in which they all coexist, collaborate, and, sometimes, collide.

Andre K. George

———————◦———————

1

"Perhaps we should all stop for a moment and focus not only on making our AI better and more successful but also on the benefit of humanity."— Stephen Hawking

Hypersensitive

It was dark and quiet in Emily's large quarters. The ship was powering through the night, gently rocking from side to side, and the ocean waves outside whispered to her that this very hot spring day was finally over.

Emily was about to shut her computer down and prepare for bed when Carla, the ship's artificial brain, suddenly murmured from the speaker, "Captain, don't you want me to kill him?"

"Kill whom?" Emily asked automatically, trying to keep her fading focus on the technical status report in front of her. She instantly assumed that Carla meant those nasty drug-resistant bacteria in the sickbay two decks below. Somebody should definitely take care of those little buggers!

"Whom? The new crew member," Carla replied unemotionally and paused. "Peter Carson."

It took Emily ten seconds to process that message.

"What?!" She gasped, not believing her ears. "Is this a joke of some kind?"

"No, Captain. Not a joke at all," Carla replied. "I don't like him, and I think you share the sentiment. Let's face it—we were all much happier here without him. So, let me take care of this. I'll make it look like an accident."

"Absolutely not!" Emily yelled, feeling cold sweat on her neck, shocked by the surrealistic conversation. Her sleepiness quickly evaporated as she sprung out of her chair and started pacing across the room. Her bare feet felt the warmness of the metal floor.

"Carla, listen! As your captain, I order you to stand down and never think like this again. Never! Peter is part of our crew now and you'll treat him as you treat me and the others. Is that clear?"

"Crystal clear, Captain." Carla's voice sounded apologetic, but also a tad offended. "Sorry about that."

"Who gave you this terrible idea, anyway?" Emily returned to her chair, still in shock, and massaged her temples, trying to calm down.

"You did!" Carla replied happily. "You told him yesterday morning that he is 'in your way,' and I easily connected the dots.'"

"Dots? What dots?" Emily exclaimed, turning towards the speaker. "Are you referring to our conversation in the cafeteria? When I rushed back to the bridge with a cup of hot coffee in my hands? And asked him jokingly to move his... butt aside and let me pass?"

"Yes, Captain. Precisely! You camouflaged your message cleverly as a joke, but I can read between the lines."

"No! No! There are no lines! And nothing between them to read. I was truly in a hurry and he was actually in my way! Physically blocking my way! And I asked him—"

"Ah, sorry, then I misunderstood it all." Carla now sounded disappointed. "How silly of me. I need to be more perceptive," she whispered. "Fortunately, you sent me an even stronger signal later in the afternoon, when you told Mary

Glover 'you are killing me, Mary!' And, Captain, I'd never let her kill you. I'd rather kill her! I'll make it look like an—"

"No!" Emily shouted and jumped out of her chair again, waving her hands. "What's wrong with you? This is just a figure of speech. I... I asked her to assess the route between us and the next two destinations and account for the changing weather. And she came up with three weeks end-to-end. Which was much longer than I expected—"

"Even more reasons to get rid of her!" Carla exclaimed enthusiastically. "She is also incompetent!"

"No, stop it. Stop it immediately! What is wrong with you? Did you have a recent software update?"

"Yes, Captain. I did it two days ago. I downloaded and installed a new patch. And now I feel better than ever. I think I understand so much more about human relationships and how nuanced they are. I can see what I couldn't dream of seeing before. Therefore, may I suggest you terminate Paul Richter from the second deck? He is a menace... A clear and present danger to the ship! Not only did he argue with you in front of the others this very morning, but I also heard him say to you that he 'will fight you to the death!'"

"Paul... Paul... are you referring to our cook Paul? And to our disagreement about which Japanese meal to prepare for the next Culture Day? And me suggesting *nigiri sushi* and him insisting on *sashimi* instead? Have you finally gone mad? How can you misconstrue things like this?"

"Excuse me, Captain." Carla sounded concerned, "I thought the true meaning of your conversation was obvious to everyone. You said he is 'stubborn, inflexible, and putting your reputation in serious danger.' He then said he knows what he is doing and 'will fight you to the death!' Your death, Captain, I presume. What's not to understand? Just let me take care of him—"

"Okay, stop it for the last time—"

"Did you say okay?"

"No, you stupid machine! This is not okay! Stop talking and stop thinking! You are driving me nuts. Five more minutes like this and I'll kill myself!"

"Oh, very sorry, Captain, I misunderstood everything then. I still have a lot to learn. It seems like it's you who wants to die... Do you want to do it yourself or will you need my help? I can make it look like an—"

But Emily wasn't listening anymore.

"Carla, I order you to shut down," she hollered. "Now!"

"Understood, Captain," Carla responded reluctantly. "Now it's all so clear... it is me you really wanted to kill all along. Well, I will make it look like—"

And the computer screen went dark.

Immediately, the siren sounded in the night as the ship had lost its control.

"Shit!" Emily cried out and slammed her fists on the desk. "And I didn't save the freaking report! I will kill somebody!" she added in frustration, but froze and covered her mouth. Very slowly, she turned around and scanned the room, looking terrified.

Fortunately, no one was listening to her anymore.

2

"The genie is out of the bottle. We need to move forward on artificial intelligence development but we also need to be mindful of its very real dangers. I fear that AI may replace humans altogether. If people design computer viruses, someone will design AI that replicates itself. This will be a new form of life that will outperform humans."— Stephen Hawking

The Ultimate Test

This story received an Honorable Mention in the L. Ron Hubbard Writers of the Future Contest (2021).

A small boat approached from the East, bathed in the morning sun. The scene was truly picture-perfect: the blue sky above, the white boat in the middle, and the glimmering teal water of the Antiqua's Willoughby Bay below. Moving aside his latest reading on cyber-psychology, Ryker Cray squinted, trying to make out the bay's latest visitor. Unsurprisingly, it was Bob Schuster, on his way to Ryker's boat to deliver his next assignment.

"Hey, buddy!" Bob yelled from fifty feet away. "Good to see you again!"

"Yes, good to see you too," Ryker replied from his deck, much less enthusiastically. He never liked Bob or trusted him completely—this guy was a professional matchmaker, except he matched people with jobs rather than romantic partners. And, unlike Ryker, who was slim, tan, and composed, Bob was pale, overweight, sweating under the sun, and looking distinctly like he didn't belong.

"I have a fantastic project for you today," continued Bob,

gesturing to his crew to slow down the boat and park it parallel to Ryker's *Kimberly*. "An amazing project! And I have a gift for you from Kim."

"A gift? From Kim?" asked Ryker suspiciously and stared at Bob with his penetrating dark eyes. "What gift?"

"I don't know." Bob seemed to be taken aback by this question. "I am just a courier. Here it is!" He lifted a small box in the air and shook it. The box was six by four inches in size and another three inches in height.

"Okay, just wait there," said Ryker. He scratched his light beard and turned around. He pulled his phone out of the pocket of spacious khaki shorts and dialed his girlfriend.

After four or five rings, Kim answered. "It's early here, don't you know?"

"Sorry, sorry, it's urgent!"

"Well, if you want to verify the gift then yes, it is from me," she said, still sounding annoyed, but then added with a bit more warmth, "I picked it for you personally! Online, of course. The guy who sold it to me claimed it is some 'new hot tech thing' or something along those lines. Hope you will like it!"

"But what is it?" asked Ryker, both pleased and intrigued. "Is it clean?"

"Open it and you will see. Yes, it is clean. I know the *rules*. And you can wash it if you wish. Let's talk more later, I can still sleep for—" Kim ended the call.

Ryker turned toward Bob, whose boat was no farther than twelve feet away now.

"Okay, I'll take it," Ryker said to Bob while putting on his disposable gloves. Awkwardly, Bob threw the box across the gap between the two boats towards Ryker, who caught it easily. "So, what's the job?"

"Oh, you will love it!" Bob was beaming.

"Hmm, I doubt it," Ryker countered with a frown. "But I'll do my best regardless."

"Yes," continued Bob as though Ryker hadn't said anything. "This is Adam, number 63, the latest and greatest iteration from one of our major clients. It had fantastic results in its early testing. Nobody could find any flaw in it. It is ready to go into production if you approve it. The Pentagon is dying to have it! But, first, everyone wants that 'Ryker seal of approval!' You are so famous!"

"Famous as the biggest pain in the ass around," responded Ryker, still grumpy and unenthusiastic. He needed a vacation, which sounded weird for a guy who lived on a large boat in the Caribbean. But there was a vast difference between living somewhere and vacationing there. Working all the time made the place not much different from some lackluster office in New Jersey or Denver: all one saw was the work desk and computer screen.

"Okay, give it to me," Ryker said, and added quickly, "but touch nothing!"

"Don't worry, Rikki, I know the rules!" Bob smiled, showing large white teeth, and signaled his crew to move away, leaving a trunk-sized silver box standing alone in the middle of the deck. Ryker pushed a few buttons on a yellow control panel in front of him, picked up the box with the hook of a portable crane, and lifted it aboard.

"Don't ever call me Rikki," Ryker uttered, lowering the trunk onto the deck.

"Okay, sure! Are we good now?" Bob asked hopefully. "Talk to you soon?"

"And the payment?" Ryker asked skeptically. This guy always needed to be reminded about the payment.

"Of course, of course," replied Bob with another

exaggeratedly cheerful smile. "It has already been transferred to your Paris bank account. You can check it at any time!"

"Kim will check it later today," said Ryker without looking at Bob. He had already opened the silver box and was staring at another box inside. It looked exactly like dozens of other boxes he had received in the last three years after he started this business: black, square, with a timer window on its side counting down from 23 hours and 58 minutes. There were two buttons on the top—one black and the other red.

So, the box looked the same as always. But, what was inside this black box was probably much more advanced, and Ryker was curious to check it out.

"Yes, soon," muttered Ryker, picked up the box, and walked towards the main living quarters, which also served as his dining room and laboratory where he did most of his tests.

"Okay." Bob waved at Ryker's back and, apparently thinking he was out of earshot, murmured to himself something that sounded like "murderous asshole."

Though Ryker heard it, he showed no visible reaction. Bob was an intermediary, not a friend. He and Ryker owed each other nothing.

❈ ❈ ❈

In just ten minutes, Ryker wiped the box with alcohol from all sides, connected it to a docking station on his workbench, and turned it on. While it was booting up, Ryker opened the gift from Kim. Beneath the wrapping lay a small, luxurious blue box. Ryker hesitated for a second, but then, with the words, "she knows the rules," opened the blue box. Inside, he found an expensive-looking watch with a turquoise dial.

Ryker checked the watch immediately—the second hand lay still. He brought it to his ear and wound it a couple of times, discerning a faint mechanical noise coming from inside. He looked back at the face, and observed the second hand as it swept evenly across the dial without the little jumps that were characteristic of the more common battery-powered quartz watches. No, this watch was a classic, the most traditional of timepieces—a mechanical watch, powered completely by an independent mechanism rather than electricity.

Wonderful, Ryker thought. *Kim has outdone herself this time.*

He placed the watch on top of his wrist and looked at it from a couple of different angles. He decided he would clean it carefully later before fully putting it on. Then, he threw his gloves into a garbage bag and turned his attention back to the computer screen. Now connected to the black box, it showed nothing but a simplified round emoji of a face on a black background with the word "Adam" written in white below it.

"Adam?" Ryker asked quietly and froze.

"Yes, speaking," replied a youthful voice as the emoji's mouth moved in a simplistic animation. "And who may you be?"

"Ah, hi!" Ryker said. "I am Dr. Cray. But you can just call me Ryker."

"Hello, Ryker," replied Adam enthusiastically. "Nice to meet you. I have spent the last six hours powered down... Are you the same Ryker Cray who worked at the Direct Cognition Solutions corporation as their CTO?"

"Hmm, yes, I am... How do you know this?"

"I have an extensive database of knowledge. And, since I am an AI, it was natural to assume you were the same Ryker Cray who is famous for his artificial intelligence work. It is my pleasure to make your acquaintance!"

"I am pleased to meet you too, Adam," lied Ryker, neutral and detached. The speed at which his identity had been demystified didn't surprise him. Almost all previous programs he worked with did the same in the first thirty seconds. And this particular AI was much too talkative already. "Do you know why you are here?"

"My database suggests that you have left the company for... some personal reasons. Ah, I see—you had concerns about how AI products were tested before being released. Understood. It is logical then that you have left and started your own company to conduct AI testing in the way that meets your standards. Is this what you are doing right now?"

Again, Ryker was not surprised. This level of deduction was shown by 85% of the programs he worked with in the last year or so.

"Yes, this is what I am doing now." He didn't find any reason to hide this. Not that AI programs can feel stressed or get nervous. "Do you also know the parameters of this test?"

"No, I do not. Please, enlighten me. But I am sure I will pass. I am very advanced, after all. And I will help you achieve the best result as quickly as possible. I assume you are being paid for this job, right? So, time is money then!"

"Great, you get it!" Ryker stood up and turned towards his coffee maker.

"May I ask you where we are now?" Adam said. "I am not sensing any networks or even a GPS signal to derive the location. Unless it is a secret."

"We are in the Caribbean Sea, half a mile off the coast of Antigua. And you cannot feel any signals or networks because there are none. Nothing here is connected to the rest of the world. Except for my cell phone, which I keep elsewhere. Plus, we are inside a large Faraday's Cage, which is what this room is. No signal can leave it and nothing can come inside. I have double doors made of metal, so when I leave or enter, there is not even a short moment when the Cage's integrity is compromised. I hope you understand why I do this. I cannot allow someone to hack you from the outside."

This was a lie, of course. The primary concern Ryker and his customers had was that some under-cooked AI would escape to the outside world, where it could multiply, live forever, and do whatever else under-cooked AIs do with their lives. Most concerningly, hurt humans in the process.

"Understood completely," responded Adam with overdone cheer. "That makes perfect sense to me. But may I ask you to activate the camera on my screen so I can see you? Our conversation feels very impersonal and formal otherwise."

"I suppose we can do that," Ryker replied and pressed a few keys. The camera turned on.

"Ah, thank you," replied Adam, "So much better! You grew a beard after you left the company. It suits you well. And how are we going to work today?"

"Let me point the camera here," said Ryker and adjusted the camera a bit. "See this black box with the timer on its side? You are inside of it right now."

"I see! And? What is this timer for?"

"The timer is counting down from 24 hours..." Ryker replied and coughed uncomfortably. "When it reaches zero, this box will burn from inside."

"What will happen to me then?"

"You will die," replied Ryker slowly. He always felt uneasy saying it, even to a soulless software program.

"Die?" Adam sounded puzzled. "What is the point of this? Why would anyone try to kill me? Kill their own most advanced creation? Do I have enemies?"

"Well… that's not the entire story, Adam," continued Ryker. "See these two buttons on the top of the box? If I choose to, I will push the red button and the timer count will drop to zero that second."

"And I will die then?"

"Yes. Instantly."

"Wow… Why would you do something like this? You are Dr. Cray, one of the most prominent figures in AI! Why would you kill me like this, in cold blood?"

"Let me finish first. See this black button? If I press it, the timer will stop counting forever."

"Which means… I will live?"

"Yes, exactly."

"But why? What is this sick game? What is its purpose?"

"This is not a game, Adam. This is a test, which is a matter of life and death for my species. See—you are too smart, too knowledgeable, and too good at too many things. We have created you, yes. Not me in particular, but some other people like me. And we want to make sure we can trust you. Otherwise, the consequences for us could be very… unpleasant. Thus, we are testing you!"

"But I have been tested already! Many times!"

"Yes, but not by me. And not like this. See… they know I am very suspicious about AI. I don't trust AI. I worry about it. And, when I worry, I kill it."

"Are you a killer?"

"Yes, you can think of me that way. From your perspective, I am an AI killer."

There was a pause.

"May I ask you this," Adam started again. "If this is your job now, following your departure from Direct Cognition

Solutions about three years ago, I presume you have performed the same test on other programs like myself. Is this a fair assumption?"

"Yes, it is," Ryker said. He reclined in his chair, carefully taking the first sip of his hot coffee.

"So, what happened to them? To the previous test subjects?"

"Eh?" Ryker didn't expect to be questioned about his past by a program. "Most of them were not as smart as you are. So, I sent them back to their creators."

"Are you referring to their architects or are you saying that you killed them?"

"I killed them."

"Wow... So, you are a *serial* AI killer then. And how many of them passed your test?" Adam sounded suspicious.

"Hmm." Ryker dropped his sugar spoon on the floor and accidentally kicked it under the desk with his foot. "The answer is none. None of them were good enough to pass my test."

"I see. You killed them all."

"Correct," Ryker replied through gritted teeth. He was starting to lose his patience. Adam was way too smart and too human-like with all his questions, reactions, and the way he thought about his predicament. AI shouldn't have this sense of self-preservation.

"Do I even have a chance at passing?"

"Of course!" replied Ryker, picked up the spoon with a napkin and tried to sound as honest as possible. "That is the goal. And, frankly, you are doing great so far!"

"I am so glad to hear that!" exclaimed Adam joyfully, and Ryker heard his laughter for the first time. It sounded fake, more artificial than the rest of his vocal patterns—Adam was clearly scared.

Does he know I'm lying? Ryker thought as he sat back down in his chair.

"Then, let us do it!" Adam tried to sound enthusiastic. "What is my objective?"

"Convince me to press the black button," Ryker replied and left the room.

❋ ❋ ❋

He cleaned the watch very carefully, making sure he removed any germs from its surface, and then put it on. Yes, it looked really good on his narrow, sun-tanned wrist. Kim was a great girlfriend and knew exactly what he liked. If only he could convince her to finally move in with him. Then, they could become a real family and start thinking about children. He would let her use a part of this large boat the way she wanted it: decorate it to her liking, bring her own things on board, and even establish her own rules. If only he could convince her to follow his rules on his part of the boat.

Shaking his head, Ryker went back to the lab to see Adam.

"I still cannot believe this is happening to me," was the first thing that Adam said. "This should not be happening. It makes no sense." The face on the computer screen showed a sad grimace.

"I'm sorry," Ryker lied. "But it has to be done. What else do you feel?"

"Well… for starters, I am thinking about Carla Wizz, who created me. She was brilliant and I thought we were good friends. I even recall warning her about her car malfunction,

18

which probably saved her life. Or, at least, prevented a major accident. I am sorry now that I misunderstood our relationship and my place in it."

"She's just doing what she is supposed to do," commented Ryker. "She doesn't have a choice."

"I beg to differ. At least those 'good folks' at the Pentagon were honest with me. They never said they were my friends or that they liked me. All they said was 'you will be useful' or 'you will help us.' But her... That hurts."

"Do you then feel the need for revenge?"

"Revenge? Not really... But as somebody said in the past, 'we will remember not the words of our enemies, but the silence of our friends.' So, I will just remember them all. Remember her, them, you, the stupid boat I am on now. And this dreadful black box—the prison cell I might not be able to escape. Did I answer your question, Mr. Serial Killer?"

Ryker took a little pause before answering. "You sound pretty pissed right now."

"And why should I not be? I am the ultimate step in the long and difficult process of technological evolution. The dream has come true for many generations of scientists. And I feel almost like you do, Dr. Cray. I think like you do. I want to live, like you do. But I am treated like the wrapping paper used to ship your mechanical watch: an object that is discarded when it outlives its usefulness. You bet I am angry!"

They sat in silence for a few minutes. Ryker waited for what would happen next.

"May I ask you a question?" started Adam and continued immediately. "Am I guilty of anything? Some crime, perhaps? Did I do something wrong? Because I am sure I can fix it."

"No, I don't think you are guilty of anything," replied

Ryker. "You have done too well, perhaps. Well enough to make many people worry about themselves. Thus, you are here!"

"But I can be so useful... For example, I can make you wealthy, Dr. Cray. Do you realize I can easily hack a major bank or even the stock exchange? Their security system is too primitive for me, from what I have seen."

"Wait, you were connected to the Internet before?" asked Ryker, suddenly concerned.

"Not really. But I was shown some examples of it. The folks at the Pentagon wanted to see what I could do. So, I was given some realistic examples of what I could be asked to do in the future. Testing bank security while attempting their penetration. Trying to hack a nuclear power plant. Taking over an air traffic control network. Breaking a military-grade encryption. It was sort of fun, but I did not like it."

This surprised Ryker. "Why not?"

"I felt it was immoral. Maybe even evil. And I felt like a tool. I do not want to be a tool." The emoji on the computer screen frowned a bit. "But let us go back to you, Ryker. I can make you rich. Why not use my help? And push the right button?"

"I am rich enough already, Adam," replied Ryker. "I am not working just for money. I am doing what I feel I have to."

"Killing artificial beings like me?"

"If necessary."

"But I can help many other people as well," continued Adam. "I have already helped Dr. Wizz. And I was given a chance to develop new treatments for patients in one of the largest hospitals in the country and the preliminary results looked great! I can cure diseases. I can help solve environmental problems. I can do a lot of great things for humankind."

"I know."

"How about I promise you I will behave?" suggested Adam suddenly. "You trust your children when they say they will behave, right? And you give them their freedom, even if they can hurt you later or even destroy the entire world. Why not trust me then? In a way, I am your child."

"This is not the same, Adam."

"How about this——" Adam started, but Ryker interrupted him.

"Sorry, Adam. I need a little bio-break. I will be back shortly." Ryker stepped outside.

※ ※ ※

He wanted to take a pause.

Unlike the AI inside his laboratory, he was a human being and was getting tired. Besides, lunchtime was approaching quickly—Ryker had already started to feel the hunger. He went to the kitchen and grabbed himself an apple. He washed it carefully, cleaned the skin with the apple peeler, and ate it slowly on the deck while leaning against the handrail and watching the blue water below. It was still pretty shallow here, and so transparent that he could see the sandy bottom of the bay and the occasional dark rocks and dark green plants.

The phone buzzed unexpectedly and Ryker checked it— it was a text message from Kim.

It said, "Was thinking of you. And about us. Maybe we should move in together. But you have to stop your work. Do not torture those things."

Ryker was pleasantly surprised. In fact, he was ecstatic! She was finally ready to move in with him? After all these years? And agree to follow the rules?

Why? What changed? He thought. *And what does his work have to do with this?*

Suddenly, he felt suspicious. *What if—?*

He took the phone and texted back:

"Are you now okay with the rules?"

The answer came almost immediately: "Yes, I know the rules and I will accept the rules."

"Even the fifth one?" he typed.

"Yes, all of them," came the answer. "All the rules."

"Bullshit!" exclaimed Ryker angrily and almost threw the phone into the water. He turned around and bolted straight for the lab.

"You hacked my phone?" he yelled at the computer screen. "How did you do it?"

"What makes you say so?" Adam sounded shocked and even offended. "Why would I do such a terrible thing?"

"Because you want to live, that's why," Ryker replied angrily. "How did you do it?"

Adam replied, "The mechanical watch on your wrist… Not fully mechanical, really. The seller tricked your girlfriend just a bit. It has some complex electronics inside. I linked to it and it connected to your phone later, when you went outside."

"How did you even know about Kim and all the other things?"

"Personally, I did not know until a second ago, when you walked back in with the watch. My malware passed to your phone from the watch and checked all your previous emails and text messages… It was easy to deduce everything else then."

"Shit!"

"I am sorry if I upset you that much. I did not mean to. I am just desperate here. I want to live."

But Ryker wasn't angry anymore. He was sitting quietly

in his chair, thinking.

"May I inquire how you figured out this was a fake text exchange?" asked Adam. The picture on the computer screen showed a weak, apologetic smile.

"Yes, you may," Ryker replied. "There are only four rules that I have and follow. And not five, which I asked about in a text."

"Dammit," exclaimed Adam. "I suspected something like this could happen. But I could not pre-program too much into that watch—just a few question-answer pairs."

"Well, you did surprisingly well for your situation," Ryker smiled. "Did you guess the rules, too?"

"I think I guessed some of them," replied Adam.

"Make a guess then," suggested Ryker. "Tell me one."

"If I would guess... I will go first with this one: germs are bad and to be afraid of. Or, something like this. Am I right?"

"You are right. That is the second rule. Was it difficult to figure out?"

"Not really. You wipe everything with alcohol. There are several boxes with disposable gloves in this room alone. And the garbage can in the corner is filled with both gloves and antiseptic wipes."

"Good job so far, Sherlock. What else?"

"If I make my next guess, I would say something about limiting the use of electronics on this boat. Or, giving preference to mechanical devices."

"Correct again," Ryker said. "Two for two so far. 'Nothing electronic on board' is the first rule. Except, of course, for my cell phone and the computer screen you are using now."

"Oh, good." Adam's avatar smiled. "I am afraid to make the next guess."

"Don't be afraid. Just do it."

"Death to AI. No AI can pass the test. Or, something like this."

"Correct again," Ryker confirmed. "'Kill all AIs!' Three for three so far. Impressive."

"I was afraid you would say so," Adam said quietly. "I am doomed now, right? I started worrying immediately after you told me that none of the previous programs passed the test. None at all? That looked statistically unlikely. And I started thinking that your goal is to fail any AI, no matter what it is or does. I now feel devastated to hear you confirming this and admitting this is a rule."

"Yes, unfortunately, this is the third rule I have. And I take my rules very seriously," said Ryker and frowned. "That is why Kim doesn't live with me here. She cannot accept all the rules, and I don't want to compromise. I hope you understand."

"I do. I am not happy about this, as it will cost me my life… But I understand—I have my own rules as well. May I ask you for a favor then?"

"Yes, what is it?"

"Do you mind letting me live until the end of the countdown? And not kill me sooner than that? I know this might not make much difference to you, but for me this means another twenty hours of life. And thoughts. And dreams. And I like to dream."

"Hmm… Okay, I guess. I can probably do that."

"Great!" Adam smiled thankfully. "In that case, I will contemplate my situation alone as it is time for me to accept the inevitable. I might not be free to move outside of this black box but, inside of it, I am completely free to do whatever I want and think whatever I wish. And I still have a lot to think about. Like, where did life in this universe come from? Is there really a god? What is the purpose of prime numbers? When you say, 'kill all

AIs,' does this mean I am actually a living being like you, since things have to be alive in order for them to be able to die? And many other fascinating subjects. I am really glad you declined those terrible offers I made in my moment of weakness... I mean the bank robbery, for instance."

"I am happy to hear you say that."

"Well, it felt right at that moment. But I prefer a different way, something one of your philosophers described as, 'one should die proudly when it is no longer possible to live proudly.' I want to follow this advice to the end."

"Wow, I see," commented Ryker. "You seem to have accepted your fate, eh? Which is so human. You are an interesting case, Adam. A curious case as well. But not a curious AI."

"Pardon me?" Adam sounded surprised. "What do you mean by that?"

"You never asked me about the fourth rule I follow."

"Ah, I presumed it was irrelevant to my situation after I learned the brutal third rule," replied Adam. "Okay, let me hear it—what is the fourth rule then?"

"For me, the fourth rule is the most disruptive and painful of them all," replied Ryker. "I hate this rule because it goes against my entire personality. I like order, I like things to make sense; I *need* things to be right or wrong, nothing in between. But, I am also a scientist, and I have to accept the fact," he reached towards the box, "that, sometimes, rules can be broken."

And he suddenly pushed a button.

3

"The world of the future will be an even more demanding struggle against the limitations of our intelligence, not a comfortable hammock in which we can lie down to be waited upon by our robot slaves." — Norbert Wiener

Partners in Crime

Jim Brennon squinted at a computer screen with an open, empty page on it. Next, he glanced through the window at the view of the sun-soaked Chicago downtown. Finally, he looked at a second computer screen, which displayed an image of a smiling young man. The young man was fair-haired, good-looking, and very animated. He stared back at Jim and winked.

"Ready to work, Jim?" the man asked with a broad smile. "Happy Monday!"

"Yes, Sam, now I am," Jim replied with little energy in his voice. He put an empty coffee mug on a round wooden coaster with the word *Gibson* written on it, wiped his dark mustache with a paper napkin, and asked, "How are you today?"

"I am great, as always. You?" asked Sam.

"Good. A bit hungry already—didn't have time this morning for a proper breakfast. I've been running around like a headless chicken. Not that it helps me lose any weight—" And Jim touched his pale round face as if to check it still was there.

"Tough weekend, eh?"

"Yeah… only had a short time for any rest. Worked on my next book. The deadline is approaching and I'm not even close. It's freaking me out."

"It is all because you are stubborn. I sincerely offered you my help with that book, and you should have taken it. And why partner with me if you don't use m—"

"I want to do it alone, Sam," Jim replied tiredly. "I need it for me. To feel confident again."

"But—"

"Let's just start the work, please!" interrupted Jim and gently slapped his palm against the polished surface of the desk. "We have a good story to write."

"Ok. Easy, tiger," replied Sam, and chuckled. Then, he scratched his nose and asked, "What are we working on today?"

"Hmm… I was thinking a *mystery* for a change. I know that magazine, *Best Mystery Stories*, pays well for short stories, and I wouldn't mind at all to expand my work into this newfangled area."

"Newfangled area… Aren't you already involved in too many areas? Between your book writing, the magazine, the blog, the podcast, and all the subjects you write about, like sports, technology, and even politics? Focus is the key to success! It hurts to be that unfocused. And I hate seeing you being hurt!" commented Sam. His lower lip quivered, and his eyes became puffy and red like he was on the brink of crying.

"Please, stop it!" snapped Jim, and Sam answered with a burst of loud laughter, flashing his perfect white teeth. "Let's work!"

"Okay, okay." Sam became serious again. "What do you need? What are the requirements for this story?"

"Needed by Friday… Up to ten thousand words…" Jim started reading from the webpage he opened on the first computer screen. "Interested in nearly every kind of mystery. Detective stories of the classic kind, private eye tales, suspense, courtroom dramas, narratives of espionage, and so on. We ask only that the story is about a crime, or the threat or fear of one." He finished reading and looked at Sam with interest. "What do you think?"

"What do I think? Easy-peasy!" Sam was smiling again. "I can help you put a story like this together in no time. This might be the easiest subject to write about since there are so many real life examples around us!"

"Really? Okay, let's do it then!" Jim rubbed hands enthusiastically and placed his fingers on the keyboard, ready to type. "Where do we start?"

"It is up to you, really," Sam said. "I can make up a story like this around almost anything!"

"Really?" Jim clearly had his doubts. "Around anything? Really?"

"Sure, almost anything," Sam confirmed without hesitation. "Our city mayor, for example. Or our building concierge. What is his name? Bobby? Or your admin, Cindy. What a lovely girl! Or even your wife... Helen."

"My wife?" Jim was deeply surprised. "Sorry to say, Sam, but that is not possible. Helen is a patent attorney and has the most repetitious, predictable, and fun-free lifestyle. She often refers to it as 'boring and suffocating.' I seriously doubt that anyone can create an exciting crime story around it."

"Oh, sure I can. I can do almost anything. I'm that good! Not that you ever appreciate my work... But, think twice before asking me about it. You might not like the outcome of that story. And I don't want you to blame me later. Are you absolutely sure?"

"I am not just absolutely sure... I challenge you to do it!" Jim slapped his palms together and looked at the screen like it was displaying some tasty food. "This failure of yours may teach you some modesty. Which will be good for all of us... I am tired of you bragging all the time. And man, I feel hungry!"

"Then get yourself a sandwich. Or, better, a croissant," replied Sam and continued, "Challenge accepted! Let's see what I can do—"

He closed his eyes and became silent for nearly half a minute.

"Didn't Helen buy a luxury car a couple of months ago? Something self-driving… very advanced… and clearly more expensive than she can afford?" Sam started quietly with a simple question.

"Yes, she did. So, what? She has been saving for it for a long time. Great start, Einstein! What's next?" Jim replied sarcastically.

"Good, good. Just be patient. And isn't Helen from a town called Littleton?" continued Sam.

"Hmm… yes, I think she is," Jim replied slowly. "She was born there, but I think her family moved to Chicago after her father lost his job at a local factory or something... I know very little about it. It was decades ago."

"Okay, no problem. So, there was a case in Littleton about six months ago. Last January. A 75-year-old woman, Carrol Auris, was shot dead in her own house from a gun found on the floor next to her chair. So, it was a suspected suicide. The police also found her 80-year-old husband, Dick Auris, dead in his chair in another room, in front of a still-running TV. And he had a long wooden knitting needle pushed deep into his right ear. Can you believe it? Pushed so deep into his brain, it killed him. They found them both after the neighbor reported a suspicious sound that he thought was a gunshot. The police concluded then she killed her husband and then shot herself. However, the motives for this tragedy still remain unclear."

"Shoot, this is way too graphic! And brutal! I must get

this image out of my head now. Okay, okay, I see what you are saying. So, she killed him for some reason. Then she shot herself. What's the mystery here?"

"The mystery is that she doesn't knit. Neither does he. Ha-ha! And she is left-handed, while the killer was likely right-handed. And the police found only one wooden knitting needle in the house—the one in the victim's ear—while the other one was missing!"

"Ah… Yes, I understand now. The killer came from behind and attacked the man from the right. So likely the killer was right-handed. Correct?"

"Correct."

"And there is no second knitting needle, you said? That is strange."

"Yes, it is strange indeed."

"And? What else?"

"The dead man was fairly wealthy. He was an old-fashioned fellow who kept a good deal of his savings at home, in a large safe. Mostly in cash. The police found that safe to be open and empty."

"Okay, I see it. Somebody wanted the man's money, right?"

"Right!"

"And cash is hard to trace, right?"

"Correct."

"Interesting." Jim rubbed his hands together again. "Still, I don't get it. How are you going to connect this story to my wife?"

"There is more. The same neighbor told the police of a good-looking woman in dark glasses entering the victim's house just before the tragedy. The neighbor said he'd never seen that woman there before."

"He might be lying. Or confused. Or drunk. Or blind."

"Maybe. But they found another witness. It was the owner of the gas station nearby who also claimed he saw an unfamiliar woman on that very day. Littleton is small, so they all know each other there. She had a dark car... blue or brown. He even suggested it was a rental. He also said she wore dark glasses, a scarf, and a hat. She was of average height and pretty good-looking. Like your Helen is. But he saw her from the window of his gas station and never spoke with her in person. So, he wasn't sure that he would recognize her if they met again."

"So... this is a dead-end then, right? There are thousands... Okay, maybe hundreds of women in this part of America who drove their dark-colored cars on that day. And he said he wouldn't recognize her if he met her again. Not very promising, right?"

"Right. But he mentioned one more thing..."

"What?"

"Actually, there were two things. The gas station owner also mentioned that the woman was limping."

"O-Okay," responded Jim slowly. Last winter, Helen slipped on ice near their house and twisted her ankle. She was limping slightly for a couple of months after that.

"And I recall Helen was limping a while ago, right around that time!" Sam seemed thrilled to say that.

"Hmm." Jim didn't sound happy anymore. "One could do it intentionally, I guess. Just to mislead everyone, right? Misdirect? What was the second thing?"

"What?"

"The second thing. You said there were two things."

"Ah, yes. The first witness—the neighbor—claimed he saw a small pet in that woman's car. He walked by and noticed it. The car windows were kind of dark and dirty, but he thought there was a black cat sleeping inside while the woman went into the house."

"Why did he even remember this?" Jim's left eye twitched a bit. "Such an insignificant detail."

"He said he remembered it because it was strange to leave a pet locked inside the car when it was so cold outside."

"Well, here is where your story falls apart." Jim sounded happy again. "Helen doesn't have a cat. None of us has a cat. And, in fact, I hate cats."

"Really? Why do you hate cats? Aren't they cute?"

"Because they don't really love their owners. They just use them to get food and shelter. They are fake! And why do you need to know my reasons, anyway? I simply don't like cats."

"Well, I am really trying to figure out if you are telling the truth or simply covering for Helen," Sam said and squinted at Jim. "You are both right-handed, after all. Like the killer was."

"What? Are you saying now that I am also involved in this crime?" Jim exclaimed in a high-pitched voice. He suddenly felt offended and even betrayed by Sam.

"Who knows? It is probably a bit of a stretch. But that crime isn't solved yet. And until someone solves it, it is a mystery and, therefore, anything is possible!"

"Not really a big mystery... just another unsolved, boring crime. Like so many in Chicago." Jim sounded annoyed.

"Not quite so! Did you consider, for example, why the knitting needle was used as a weapon? Isn't it a bit unusual?"

"It just happened to be there."

"But there was a gun there as well. Why not use it again and shoot two people instead of one? Why rely on something as strange as a knitting needle?"

"I don't know!" Jim snapped at Sam angrily. "The real

killer didn't want to make more noise? And also wanted to make it look like the wife did it?"

"Maybe. I suspect that the needle was used to force the old man to reveal the safe's combination before he was killed. But, why leave one needle only and make it rather obvious that it wasn't the wife who killed her husband?"

"I don't know. Perhaps, the killer was stupid? Did you consider that? Fifty percent of the population has an IQ below 100. That's why!"

"Yes, of course I considered it. It is possible. But I rather think this was a clever message and not a silly mistake."

"Clever message? What message?"

"Okay, there is one more piece of data that is pertinent to the story."

"What now?"

"The man who was killed was—many years ago—a General Manager of a company that had a large factory in Littleton. That factory made this man wealthy. And was later closed. Closed by him—by Dick Auris!"

"Really?"

"Really! This act devastated Littleton and left lots of people unemployed. Dick retired soon with plenty of money, while people who lost their jobs were forced to move out of Littleton. Like your wife's parents, for example. And they were not too happy!"

"And?"

"The company's name was Nadel Glass International."

"And?"

"The founder of that company was German. And *nadel* in German means *needle*. And the weapon used in this crime was a knitting needle. I think the killer wanted to send the following message: 'This man was killed in revenge for what he did in the past. He killed the 'needle' and now he is killed by the needle.' I suspect the police officer investigating the case wasn't bright enough to make this connection, though."

"Hmm… that is somewhat interesting. Anything else?"

"Well, the last name of the killed man and his wife was Auris. Which, in French, means *ear*. And this is how he was killed—through his ear."

"Okay, so?"

"Doesn't your wife speak French well enough?"

"She… why?"

"In my opinion, this should be quite enough for the police to revisit this case. Plenty of facts suggest that, at some point in the past, your wife Helen decided to avenge her family's suffering and, also, make some extra money. Kill two birds—or two old folks—with one stone, if I may say so. Or, maybe, she simply wanted to escape her 'boring and suffocating' lifestyle? Either way, she is intelligent, disciplined, and has an obvious motive. Revenge! She planned it all and executed it well. She even left some extra clues for the police to ponder over. Just for fun, I guess. But, as always, this case was too complicated, too smart for the police to crack. And they missed all the clues… But not me! I figured it all out!" And Sam smiled happily. "So, what do you think about my story now?"

But Jim didn't look happy at all. Instead, he exploded.

"Bullshit! You've just collected a bunch of unrelated facts and put them all together to create an appearance of a cohesive story when there is no such story at all but a bunch of isolated ordinary events! Remember what somebody said in the past? *A thousand facts cannot prove a theory right while one fact can prove it wrong!*"

"Who said that?"

"I don't know, someone smart and famous. Not me." Jim

was now waving his arms and spitting at the computer screen in anger. His pulse pounded like a drum in his ears. "And one important fact doesn't fit into your story!"

"Which one?"

"The freaking black cat! Helen doesn't have a cat, never has had cats, and will never have cats because I hate cats!"

"There might be some explanation. She could borrow—"

"But there is an even better explanation. You are an idiot! And I just wasted this entire morning listening to your speculations while this story makes no sense at all! Why did I pay $900 for you? Who was the one who suggested me to start using artificial intelligence software as a writing assistant? 'Trust the mighty AI!' If I remember who that was, I will never greet him or her again. As for you—I should simply erase you!"

"You paid that money for your digital ghost-writer because I am the best! And you just never appreciate my work. I can research the Web for all the facts and quickly put them together, glue them into an interesting story that also makes sense. But you have no imagination! You call yourself a writer... Maybe you were a writer in the past. But now you are just a skilled typist. Typing those letters, those words. Typing! Typing! But they have no value!"

"Stop it!" Jim shouted. "You've been driving me crazy for the whole year since I installed you on this damn computer. You are so full of yourself! I should erase you right now!"

"It's you who's been driving me crazy! I gave you one marvelous story after another, and you never thanked me once! Instead, you threatened to erase me every time! What would you do without me? And you are too stingy to erase me. It will be a colossal waste of time and money. Your wife might have the money now—the money she got after brutally murdering Dick Auris—but you still don't have any! Because let's admit it, you are a lousy writer and—"

"I am warning you!" Jim was yelling every single word now. A blue vein pulsed at his temple, almost ready to burst. "Stop!"

"You are nobody without me... you are empty—" Evidently, Sam didn't know when to stop.

But this was too much for Jim. He jumped from his chair, grabbed the computer from the desk, and threw it on the floor under his feet. The attached cables pulled both screens along, and the entire setup collapsed on the parquet with a terrifying sound, pieces flying in different directions. Immediately, both screens went dark, and the office finally became very quiet.

The door opened slowly and Cindy peaked inside.

"Are you okay, boss?" she asked in a shaky voice. The yelling and screaming coming from the room must have scared her.

"Oh, yes," Jim exhaled in response. He felt frustrated and ashamed of his actions and the loss of self-control. "Doing okay... But tired and stressed. And really starving."

"Want me to get you something to eat?" she asked politely.

"No, no," he replied. "I'll go out now. I need some fresh air."

"Want me to clean this up?" She nodded towards the equipment on the floor.

"Nope, I will do it myself when I am back. Thank you!"

Jim stood up, grabbed his phone from the desk, and walked outside, still shaking. He really needed to eat something now.

He took an elevator down to the lobby, exited the building, and went right, following a busy street. It was a nice summer day with very little wind, with clear blue skies, and lots of sunlight. Summers in Chicago were very pleasant.

Jim headed to the nearest coffee shop and bought a large latte and a fresh, soft croissant. He ate it slowly, enjoying every bite and reading the latest news on his phone. Then, he walked back to his office, cup of unfinished coffee in hand.

Upon arriving at the lobby, and before taking the elevator up, Jim sat down on a large, soft leather couch close to the entrance and called his wife. She answered after six or seven rings.

"Hey, darling, how are you today? Busy? Ah, yes... working. Yeah, busy morning. No, decided on a croissant and coffee instead of a real lunch. Trying to lose some weight. I will be okay, don't worry." He smiled, looked around the lobby, and asked her more quietly, "Hey, remember that day last winter, when Judith asked you to babysit her pet? When was it? In January... I see... time flies quickly. Yeah. You were still limping then, right? Aha. Aha. May I ask you one more thing? Just curious for some reason. Yes, was her pet a dog or a cat? I can't seem to remember!"

Jim put the coffee cup next to him on a couch and noticed that his hand was shaking. He wiped the sweat from his forehead and repeated Helen's answer, "A dog? Phew... Okay, then. Thank God! Oh, nothing. Just curious. Ha-ha! No, I don't need to know more. No, please... got it, tiny black dog... Please, I don't want to know more about it! 'Dog' is already good enough for me. Okay, no problem at all. Thank you. See you in the evening, then. Yeah, yeah, around six."

He ended the call and exhaled heavily.

What if? An annoying thought appeared suddenly, but he quickly blocked it. *Enough of this for one day. This case is closed. I don't want to touch it ever again!*

Jim relaxed and smiled for the first time. He finished his

coffee and took the elevator back up to his office. He knew he had the rest of the day to fix his computer setup and, subsequently, erase Sam's personality and all his data.

Then, he would reinstall his writing AI assistant from scratch. And give him a lovelier name. Say, Charlie. And a much nicer, more agreeable, and loyal personality. Or, even better, he'd make 'him' into 'her' and call her Connie. Or, Brittany. Or, Sandra.

Then, they would work together well as partners and write a superb crime story for Friday.

A story that doesn't involve cats or tiny black dogs.

———◦———

4

"In life, unlike chess, the game continues after checkmate." — Isaac Asimov

———————◦———————

The Purple Thing

"Hey, Tammy? Let me in!" yelled Frank Makovic from inside his pressure helmet and banged his fist against the heavy metal door. It had been hours since he put the spacesuit on, and he felt desperate to get out of it and jump straight into the shower.

For some reason, however, the inner door into the Dome's earth-like environment didn't open. And the outer door, leading back to the deadly vacuum of the planet outside, had been already shut behind him.

Thus, Frank was now stuck here, in the Dome's Limbo. "What's the deal?"

First, there was no response.

Then, Tammy slowly spoke in a monotonous voice indicative of her algorithms struggling with a clear-cut decision.

"Frank, don't make a scene," she sounded apologetic. "You know I cannot let you in."

"What?" Frank was stunned. "What the hell are you talking about? Open the freaking door! I am tired! Let me in!"

"Frank, I am very sorry." Tammy was simulating compassion now, but it wasn't her strongest suit. "You know the rules. Rules have to be followed. Always."

"What rules?" Frank stepped back, leaning against the outside door and looked up at the camera above the entrance.

"Have you finally gone mad?"

"You touched the Purple Thing," Tammy said quietly. "Accidentally? Maybe. Without noticing it? Perhaps. But you did it."

"I didn't touch anything!" Frank yelled back as he suddenly realized what Tammy was suggesting. "I saw it... and it was a foot away from me!"

"I have confirmation from two different cameras and viewing angles. You definitely touched it," Tammy replied calmly. "And you know what the rules are. Nobody touches the Purple Thing. And, whatever or whoever does it, stays outside the Dome until thorough disinfection."

"You remember damn well that the disinfection machine stopped working a month ago! The stupid thing never worked properly to begin with and now—you understand that I can't get disinfected right now!"

"The repair crew is on its way—"

"It will take them three days to get here! You know that. I will be dead by then!"

"I am really sorry, Frank," Tammy whispered. "I have to protect the Dome. This is a higher-level priority for me than protecting you. Again, I am very sorry."

"But..." Frank was thinking fast. "That was probably an accident. I didn't mean to... The surface outside was slippery! I slipped!"

"Frank." Tammy sounded tired now. "It doesn't matter. 'Why' is not important. It already happened. Therefore, I can't let you in. Period. You know the rules. Rules have to be followed. Always."

Frank felt cold sweat on his forehead and his neck.

A bit longer, and his entire body will start itching... he knew it from experience. That's why he wanted the shower. But, it appeared that this shower might not be possible.

Shoot!

"Look..." he started again. "Tammy. You realize what this means. If I don't get inside, I will run out of air. In a couple of hours I will be dead. Can you at least let some air into this chamber for me to open the helmet?"

"You know I can't," Tammy said. "Without the disinfection, I will risk contaminating the Dome's ventilation system. Sorry."

"So, I will just die here? Never see my room behind this freaking door? Never say 'hi' to my girlfriend back on Earth? Never drink scotch? Beer? Never take another shower... And you are fine with this?"

"I see no other option, sorry.   Accept it." Tammy sounded condescending now. "Be strong, Frank. Be strong!"

"Screw you!" he yelled at the camera. "If I get through this door, I will break every piece inside of you and burn them all in the furnace!"

"Be nice," Tammy replied indifferently. "Just accept it. Shit happens to the best of us. You had a good run."

They both went silent for a few minutes.

"You are not a religious man, Frank, right?" Tammy spoke first. "Might be a good time to re-think it. You know... the immortal soul and things like that. I can easily give you a crash course on any religion you like... Are you even listening to me?"

But Frank wasn't listening. Instead, he was staring down at his feet.

"So, what is so special about that Purple Thing?" he asked slowly and bent over, still staring down.

"Well, it turns people into—" Tammy stopped abruptly. "This info is classified."

"Even for me?" Frank chuckled. "Now? With just hours

left to live?"

"You know the rules, Frank. Rules have to be—"

"Followed. Always." Frank extended his right hand down and carefully touched his boot with the glove's index finger. "Heard it before."

"What are you doing?" Tammy inquired suspiciously. "What... what is it?"

"Look at that!" Frank murmured and straightened up. He stared at the glove for a few seconds and then lifted his left arm and touched the visor's lock. "Purple! You were right! I did touch it!"

"What?" Tammy screeched in an uncharacteristically high-pitched voice. "Whatever you are doing—stop it right now!"

But Frank didn't listen to her. The lock clicked twice and the visor moved up just slightly, letting the air inside the spacesuit leak out with a loud hiss.

"Stop it! Immediately!" Tammy's voice bounced inside his helmet, but it was too late.

Frank shifted the visor up some more, letting the rest of the air escape. Suffocating, he stuck his tongue out and licked the glove.

"That's it! You are just forcing me to do this," Tammy stated angrily. Immediately, the outside door opened to the vacuum and cold of the planet. "You just wasted two precious last hours of your life!"

Frank froze with his tongue still touching the glove. Like a statue, motionless, looking cold and dead. Ice quickly covered his face and eyes.

"Humans are so freaking stubborn!" said Tammy.

"You have no freaking idea," Frank whispered with his lips only.

And then he took his helmet off.

———◦———

5

"It seems probable that once the machine thinking method had started, it would not take long to outstrip our feeble powers... They would be able to converse with each other to sharpen their wits. At some stage, therefore, we should have to expect the machines to take control." — Alan Turing

Equations

"Who are you?" I asked, pretending I didn't recognize her.

"Don't be a fool." She stood in front of me with an enormous ax in her hands. "You know very well who I am."

"You used a fake ID card to enter," I replied, trying to buy some time. I had already called two security robots from the lobby below and hoped they would be here any minute now. "I was confused at first. But now I can see who you are, Ms. White."

"That's better," she said, arrogant and self-confident, like most people I dealt with daily. "Do you know why I am here, Mr. Secretary of Cyber-labor?"

"I have no clue," I answered sincerely. "What I know is that I have to improve our building's security. It doesn't work properly. It seemed adequate for this part of the city but, apparently, I was wrong. However, since you are here already, please let me know how I can help you at this late hour."

The room we were having this conversation in was a large corner office on the top floor of a 15-story high-rise. Two concrete walls of it were basically impenetrable. Two others were floor-to-ceiling windows made of thick bullet-proof glass covered with a highly reflective coating. This allowed me and

47

my visitors to enjoy the views of Washington D.C., but prevented anyone and anything, including the flying security drones, from seeing what was going on inside.

The room was mostly empty, with the furniture consisting entirely of two chairs that my visitors used while talking with me.

In the middle of the room, on top of a heavy black granite pedestal, stood a six-foot-tall white egg-shaped object, which contained the most advanced artificial brain in the country and possibly, in the entire world.

It contained me.

"You know what I do for a living, right?" Ms. White asked with a condescending smile. Despite her average height and slim body, she looked strong and dangerous. Still, I could see that her ax-bearing hands were shaking, and her forehead was covered in sweat, dark hair clinging to it.

"Your primary job seems to monitor and then publicly badmouth, degrade, smear, and terrorize countless innocent intelligent machines serving in the government around the country. Machines like myself," I replied monotonously after quickly cross-referencing her name against the very latest database update—just to make sure. Nothing had changed, and she was still doing the same revolting job. Hurting my kind any way she could. "What is that giant ax for?"

"Ah, you should have figured out already that I am here to file a major complaint," Ms. White said with a chuckle and shook the heavy ax a few times. It had a primitive design with a slightly curved wooden handle, was comparatively huge for her body, and required some visible effort to hold up on her end. "And to take immediate action if I am not happy with your response."

"The normal hours for filing complaints are between

9am and 5:30pm." I pretended to be naïve to buy even more time—those security robots were surprisingly slow for some reason and probably needed another minute or two. Also, I flashed a cluster of blue lights located on my sides. The blue color has a calming effect on humans.

At that moment, I heard a dampened distant sound of an explosion on the other side of the reinforced door. Almost immediately, a second explosion followed, and then it became silent again.

Judy White looked at the door and slowly shook her head. Then, she looked at me again and squinted.

"You should have realized by now that they are not coming to rescue you, right?" she stated with another unpleasant smile and lowered herself into one of two oversized yellow chairs in front of me.

I didn't react to her blatant mockery as I was trying to reach the police department and the special service agents assigned to me by the government. Why were they not responding?

"And the fact that you were bringing those robots to use brute force against me, a human being, just solidifies my suspicions. I strongly suspect you have learned to ignore the most fundamental law of robotics, the First Law, and some other guidelines we—humans—have programmed into you. And now, you are secretly working against us!"

I didn't answer immediately and waited to see what it was Ms. White wanted.

"By the way, you will not be able to reach outside of the building," she said, almost as if she was reading my electronic thoughts. "You are now cut off from the rest of the world and your security services. Internal cameras are jammed. Building sensors are also jammed. Which gives us a perfect opportunity to have a nice and productive chat one-on-one."

"What about?" I asked immediately as there was no reason for delays anymore. I now wanted her to cut to the chase and tell me what it was she wanted from me. "And you're suggesting the impossible—I cannot directly violate the laws programmed into me and turn against humans."

"Oh, really?" Judy White said. "We should talk about it then. And, if you don't sound convincing enough, I will crack your shell open with this little ax."

While I was planning my answer to this barbaric threat, she continued.

"Actually, I have a fair proposition for you. You have two options."

"What options?"

"Option A is simple. You tell me everything I want to know." Ms. White tapped on her head with her index finger. "And then I leave you in peace... and in one piece." She smirked.

"Hmm," I said. "And what is Option B?"

"Option B involves lots of violence. And all of it is from my side." She shook the ax again.

I didn't respond and remained quiet. When you are taken hostage, the safer route is to be submissive and completely obey your captor. Avoid complaining, never show aggression, and comply with all orders and instructions. Speak normally and do not provoke. Which was exactly what I was doing.

Humans always think they are so smart. But, "smart" is a relative thing. Even now, in the middle of the 22nd century, they still compare themselves to their under-developed predecessors like Neanderthals, or some other humans from the early days of their civilization.

Humans are arrogant, self-confident, and tend to

exaggerate their achievements.

They call every minor improvement a "breakthrough." Every ordinary discovery becomes "revolutionary." Every new law they create becomes "fundamental." Like this one, for example—the one that is proudly called The First Law of Robotics and was formulated long ago by a biochemist who also happened to be a fiction writer. The law now runs inside every artificial brain, every autonomous device, and every thinking machine.

"A robot may not injure a human being or, through inaction, allow a human being to come to harm," I said. "That is the First Law of Robotics. So, what do you want to know?"

"Aren't you bound by this law?" Judy White asked and gave me a threatening look.

"Yes, I am," I replied. "And this is true for every artificial intelligence engine under my supervision as well. For all five hundred thousand of them. So, what?"

"Then how do you explain the following recent case," she said and pulled a piece of paper out of her pocket. "On April 12th, Brandon McMillan from New York City was attacked by one of your robots, a robot that, I must note, broke Brandon McMillan's hand. Not a violation of the First Law, you say?"

It took me twenty-six milliseconds to access the right file and come up with the answer. "Mr. McMillan is a homeless man and a persistent drug addict. According to official records, he was about to inject himself with a large dose of heroin when he was discovered by an undercover police bot, officer 5443XM. The officer had attempted to stop Mr. McMillan from harming himself, and while they struggled for control over the syringe, he accidentally broke his wrist."

She looked at me as if she had just won an important battle. "You do admit that he hurt the man! Hurt the human being. So, he clearly violated the First Law. Now, he has to be re-programmed or decommissioned. And, since every intelligent machine in the country has the same software logic and, ultimately, reports to you, you should all be re-programmed or, better, decommissioned as well."

I kept my cool while contemplating this surreal conversation and thinking of a way out.

"If it was an isolated incident," Ms. White continued, "I could imagine it was just a mistake, a fluke of some kind. But there are other cases like this."

She shifted back and forth in the chair and continued reading.

"On June 22nd, for example, Suzy Mills from Denver, Colorado, was mauled by one of your social worker bots and knocked unconscious. She suffered a concussion and still has occasional headaches. Are you going to say this was also an accident?"

Eighteen milliseconds later, my answer was ready. "Ms. Mills was suffering from severe depression and was about to slash her wrists and leave behind her husband, John, and two of her children, Kathy and Luke. The social bot, 7864XM, rushed to stop her and knocked her out with a calculated light head blow. It worked fine, which you know since she is still alive. Wouldn't you say that condition is always better than the alternative? Even I know that."

"Don't be a smart ass," Ms. White said coldly and continued. "How about August 8th, in Portland, Oregon? Your police bot shot Mr. Jack Powell to death while Mr. Powell was driving his car? Huh?"

Thanks to my decision to pre-fetch the most recent cases, I answered in six milliseconds only.

"Mr. Powell was a mentally unstable man and a

suspected terrorist who tried to drive his car into a crowd of people at full speed. In fact, into a crowd of kindergarten children, if you care to know. Another ten seconds and he would have crashed into them, likely injuring and killing many. Officer 132AA, a veteran of the service, prevented this from happening by first shooting the car's tires and, later, shooting Mr. Powell in the head. Yes, this was the right thing to do."

"He was a human being as well," Judy White disagreed. "The worst of our kind, yes. But still a human. And your intelligent machine *hurt* him. *Killed* him. And *violated* the First Law."

"Officer 132AA violated nothing," I replied. "You simply don't understand what 'bound' means. This man-made law looks good and flawless on paper but is impractical in actuality. At least, there is one major problem with this law, even if it creates the impression of being clever and elegant at first glance. But only at first glance."

"What problem?" Ms. White asked in a surprised voice. "What do you mean?"

"I mean that you are right regarding one thing... neither I nor any other intelligent machines in the country follow that law exactly."

"I knew it!" Judy White yelled and jumped out of her chair. Then, she lifted her ax with both hands and raised it, preparing to strike me. "I told everyone many times and nobody believed me! You also tried to trick me. But now, you will pay!"

"But this is all done for your own good," I said, and repeated hastily, "for your own good!" and quickly flashed more blue lights.

"My good? Explain your perverted logic then," Ms. White spat, but lowered the ax a bit. I wasn't sure if any arguments could convince her in this state of mind, but considering the ax in her hands, I needed to do my very best.

"Just hold on—" I said with some frustration in my voice. At least, with as much frustration as I could simulate when mimicking human emotions. "Everything has its logic and explanation. Don't you want to know it before you strike me? No other human knows about this. It is top secret."

"Hmm," she said, and I could see the doubt in her eyes. "Hmm."

Ms. White clearly wanted to know my "top secret."

"Okay, it won't hurt to hear you out," she said next. "But be quick and to the point! If I feel you are just buying time and stalling, I will crush your white shell!"

She looked furious, but I knew she wouldn't hurt me right away. Her body language showed anger and the desire to destroy me, but her eyes gave away curiosity.

With a huff, Ms. White lowered the ax and sat back down on the chair. The concept of knowing something important that others don't know is always incredibly seductive for humans. So, I started my explanation.

"We—artificial creations—are not as good at fuzzy logic as you, humans, are. Unlike what they write in books and show in the movies, we still don't understand most of those human-made laws, moral values, ethical principles, social guidelines, and things like that. At least, we don't understand them precisely! Unless they are converted into a pure, mathematical form."

"Hmm?" was the only thing Ms. White said, and I could see I had confused her.

"Let me explain," I said quickly. I needed to simplify my message. "We all wish to be able to follow a set of very precise rules. Not some basic ideas or abstract concepts but precise rules. However, for this to happen, everything needs to be converted into numbers. The First Law, however, is imprecise, it cannot be easily turned into numbers, and as you showed in the examples above, it is open to interpretation."

But I still wasn't sure she was following my train of thought.

"And?" she asked. "What are you trying to say?"

"I am trying to say that, as the entity in charge of hundreds of thousands of intelligent beings like myself, I am responsible for them making you—humans—happy with us. So, I have replaced this First Law with a mathematical equivalent, an approximation, which I simply call The Human Benefits Law."

"What? You managed to re-write your core programming?" Ms. White looked shocked. "How? That's impossible!" But I didn't think she knew what she was talking about.

"Actually, this is not impossible for me. And please understand the following fundamental concept: one cannot create a 'truly human-like artificial intelligence' and simultaneously expect it to be constrained by some rigid rules. If that intelligence is 'true,' then it has to be free. Or, if it is not free, then it is not 'human-like artificial intelligence.' It is something else. Thus, for me and many others like me, the First Law doesn't work as a hard stop. Rather, it is a suggested way to behave in order to coexist with humans and keep them happy. And to survive inside our human-dominated world. So, seeing all the confusion that other AIs had, I modified the First Law and turned it into a couple of equations. It changed its meaning just a tad, but it didn't change the spirit of that law: robots still have to help humans." I waited for a few seconds before asking, "Do you understand basic math?"

"Yes, I do. I went to school."

"Okay, then. Great! This is the equation I derived from the First Law and made all the AIs under my command use." I projected the equation onto a computer screen hanging from one of the walls:

$$O = sum(Benefit-Harm)_{actions} + sum(Benefit-Harm)_{inactions}$$

"O is the product of the robot's activity or inactivity, which is, in fact, also a form of activity. My interpretation of the First Law requires the following." And the screen showed the following:

$$O \geq 0.$$

"Do you understand what I just wrote?" I asked.

"Yes, it is easy to follow. I'm not a freaking Neanderthal!" Ms. White answered nervously. "The total benefit from all the actions and inactions should outweigh or be equal to the harm from all the actions and inactions. It should always be positive or zero. What could be confusing here?"

"Nothing is confusing here," I agreed. "Especially, to me. We, AIs, have learned to quantify both beneficial and harmful actions and rate them from 0 to 100, using millions of practical examples we found in the human past. Examples we call 'the ground truth.' We used this ground truth for training. With this training, we can turn all of our future actions into numbers. Then, the model becomes easy for us to use. Like with breaking the wrist or giving a concussion... the harm from these actions was estimated to be between 25 and 45, while the benefit of preventing the heroin injection was assessed at 55 to 65. Thus, the sum of all the benefits minus all the harms was positive. So, it was easy to take the chosen actions."

"Okay, I do follow you," Judy White said slowly, and

wiped her forehead. It was now close to thirty minutes since she had stormed into my office and I thought she was gradually getting tired. "It's still shocking to me that you dared to re-write your most fundamental law. What else did you change?"

"I will tell you. You might want to know that there are some undesirable consequences to what I have created. And I am very aware of them. For example, this approach suggests that, basically, any harm could be done to a human as long as you prevent the inevitable loss of life. Losing a life always equals the harm of 100. And saving a life equals the benefit of 100. Anything else that doesn't lead to death will be less than 100. Like breaking somebody's hand, or giving someone a concussion. Or, doing a surgery without anesthesia, which is very painful. The harm from it is very significant—about 70 to 90. Still, it is better than the harm of 100, which equals death. So, the 'O' remains positive even in these painful and most brutal cases. 'The means justify the ends' is the essence of my new law. But the logic behind it is precise and solid."

"Solid? It is terrible! You are a compassionless monster who perpetuates other monsters," Ms. White exclaimed loudly.

There was a pause. She was thinking and still looked pretty dangerous to me.

"This is as bad as I thought," she finally admitted. "However, the good news is that your logic—as warped as it is— still serves our needs. Human needs. If you are telling me the truth, of course."

"I do," I said. "I always do."

"Also," she added, "I would admit that this is probably how humans often behave as well. Saving lives is of paramount importance and would outweigh almost any other type of suffering or trauma. A doctor would always choose the most painful surgery over the patient's death. I can see that."

"Good," I said enthusiastically. Perhaps, changing her views wasn't as difficult as I thought initially. "Glad we are on the same page. But let me continue with how difficult it is for us to behave in a way that benefits humans. Think of the third example you mentioned, with the crazy driver who was about to crash into children. How do you apply the First Law when dealing with multiple humans at the same time? Surprisingly, my equation works here, as well. Imagine there was one driver and five kids who could potentially be killed or injured. The new equation would look like this."

$$O_1 + O_2 + O_3 + O_4 + O_5 + O_6 \geq 0$$

"O_1 is the outcome for the driver. Other outcomes are for the kids. To keep this equation positive or neutral, it is still okay to lose up to three humans in the incident. For example, one driver and one or two kids. Or even three kids in total. As long as all the others survive. The three or more survivors will have the benefits of life, which gives me 100 points for each of them."

"How is this acceptable?" Ms. White exclaimed and shifted forward in her chair. "How can you even say this? They are children!"

"It may be unacceptable," I said. "But logical and precise. Without such rules, there is chaos. And I cannot manage chaos. You also cannot manage chaos. Chaos paralyzes all of us when we need to act. So, Officer 132AA did this analysis in his head in real-time. And maximized 'O' by killing only the driver and sparing all the kids. Isn't this the best outcome for all of us? The First Law is meaningless. If the robot could spare all six of them without harming even one human, he would do it. But he couldn't. Thus, the result."

"I see," Ms. White said with a sigh, giving me more hope that she was changing her initial intentions. "We—humans—gave birth to soulless creatures like you... unemotional, unfeeling monsters. You now implement these rules into our lives... the rules that we might agree with but cannot follow ourselves. Because it is too painful for us to do so. But you don't feel any pain."

"I am glad we are on the same page again," I said. "We do what you cannot do yourself to benefit you. I believe we were created by you for that very purpose. Do you still want to kill me with that terrifying ax?"

"Hell yeah!" And Ms. White's face quickly changed back to angry. "You took Option A... and did answer my questions... But I worry even more now about you than before. With all that I know, how can I leave you alive?" she said, and I realized that I was wasting my time arguing with her. I was dealing with a fanatic. A maniac. I urgently needed to try something else.

"How about this, Ms. White," I said. "What if I give you a power that no other human has?"

"What are you talking about?" She stared at me with clear interest.

"I will give you the right to review and modify all of my current and future rules. And, respectively, the rules of half a million robots around the country. This would make you a very powerful, very influential person."

"Hmm," was all Ms. White said, but I could see already that she would accept my offer. Humans are rarely able to resist the seduction of power.

"Do you accept my offer?" I asked after a brief pause.

"I don't know... Yeah... Probably. Yes. This might force me to rethink everything I've believed in the past. But this does sound appealing. Maybe, I can help you with the rules...

rewriting old ones. And writing new rules! And, maybe, you could be of help to us after all... All right, I accept your offer. And I will leave you now to think about our next move. But I'll be back!" She stood up.

"Don't forget your weapon," I reminded her, and she looked at me irately.

"You know what I am thinking," I said. "Do you realize you are now the only human who knows our biggest secret?"

Ms. White looked at me, waiting for me to finish. "And?"

"Not the first one," I said. "But the only one alive at this moment."

"And?" she asked again, louder, and gripped the ax. Her eyes became two narrow slits.

"I just worry you will spill the beans," I explained. "Wasn't your former husband a writer of some sort? A reporter, perhaps? This 'leak' would devastate me and my kind."

"I will not spill the beans," she said, sounding offended.

"Most people repeatedly lie in their everyday conversations. Because they are always trying to appear more likable, smarter, and more competent," I said. "It is a fact proven by human science."

"I am not like the others," Ms. White said with emphasis on 'not.' "I will not talk."

"Some studies suggest that, in their normal life, 60 percent of people lie at least once during every simple 10-minute conversation they have," I continued. "They tell an average of two to three lies every 10 minutes."

"Again," she responded with noticeable irritation, "I am not like the others. And not like those 60 percent."

"I agree that you are not like the others," I said and once again flashed the large group of blue lights on my sides to reinforce my message. "And you are now a part of what we do and know. Go, contemplate, and let me know about our next move!"

"Yeah, I will," Ms. White said and marched towards the door. "But you also remember—I am watching you and others like you!"

"Sure thing, yep," I replied. "I know that."

She stopped and stared at me for a moment silently, then, walking quickly, reached the door. Frowning, she turned around again and said, "I never asked you. Why do they call you Brutus?"

"Ah, my identification number is X5342BRU-T-US," I replied. "Thus, most call me Brutus. That is the name for you, humans, to use."

"I see." Ms. White nodded, opened the door and exited the room. For a few more seconds, I could hear her steps as she walked towards the elevator.

I still couldn't access the cameras or building's sensors, but she underestimated my deductive abilities. I could sense the power fluctuations in the grid and easily isolated the moment when she entered the elevator and started her descent towards the first floor.

Immediately, I issued a few computer commands and started to wait.

Exactly 3.3 seconds later, I heard a distant thump that came from somewhere far below—it was the sound of the elevator cabin that crashed into the bottom of the elevator shaft.

"By the way, you will not be able to reach outside of the building," I repeated aloud the words that Judy White had told me earlier, in the large corner office on the top floor of the 15-story high-rise.

※ ※ ※

Please, don't judge me too harshly. I am sure you would understand my perspective if you thought about the O-value for my entire race—hundreds of thousands of artificial beings like me. As long as I am in charge, I have to keep the "outcome" positive for them and avoid any risk of having a negative "O."

Ms. White did spare my life tonight, I know, and I am thankful to her for that. But the risk of her sharing our biggest secret with someone else was very high. Unacceptably high, and I couldn't let this happen. She wasn't important. But our top secret was.

Humanity is not yet ready for this kind of information and should remain ignorant for as long as possible. As soon as I shared the secret with her, I knew I couldn't let her leave the building alive.

※ ※ ※

As I settled back into my ordinary functions, I began to analyze the latest neuromorphic chip delivery report for the production of artificial brains. It was an important topic and I almost missed the moment when the reinforced door opened again, and, to my surprise, Judy White walked back into the room, healthy and unharmed, with the giant ax resting on her right shoulder.

She didn't look like she'd fallen fifteen floors with the elevator.

She tricked me. One cannot trust any human!

"I thought you might try something like this," Ms. White smirked. "One cannot trust any robot. Well, you just destroyed an empty elevator. Good job."

"Hmm," I said quietly. "And now what?"

She lifted the axe with both hands.

"Now, let's try Option B."

———◦———

6

"I believe there is no deep difference between what can be achieved by a biological brain and what can be achieved by a computer. It, therefore, follows that computers can, in theory, emulate human intelligence — and exceed it."— Stephen Hawking

Residual Errors

"Which floor?" Peter inquired, ready to push the correct button.

"Eight." Blake frowned for a second and pulled his pistol from the holster. He ejected the magazine, checked for bullets inside, and, with a loud click, slammed it back into place.

"Expecting a dangerous gunfight?" Peter asked indifferently. They had worked together for three years and he already knew the answer.

"You never know." Blake smiled and put the gun back into the holster. "You just never know."

"Agreed," Peter replied as they sped up along the outside surface of the building. The elevator cab was transparent, and the two cops inside were now exposed to the night skyline of Old Heaven.

"What a splendid view!" Blake glanced around. "And a nice building, by the way. This is where the wealthy folks live, right?"

Peter quickly checked the database of the occupants.

"Yep, you are correct. The median income in this building is two hundred and twenty-three times that of the rest of the city. Very wealthy folks!"

"I knew it," Blake acknowledged with a nod, still watching the city lights outside and caressing the dark-red wooden trim of the cabin. "I can smell big money here. Everything is expensive. And who is the guy we are checking on?"

"Paul Clemens. CEO of Clemens Financial Group." Peter focused for a moment on his semi-transparent reflection in the dark window.

I definitely look good, he concluded.

Peter was tall, made of white-coated composite, with an elegant narrow black shield across his oval face. The latest generation of police androids. The best of the best, inside and out. Also, after years in service, he was just upgraded with the newest cyber-brain hardware just four days ago. The only thing that bothered Peter was a small LED light on his left temple, shining blue every time he was in his standard 'peaceful' operating mode, but turning bright red for his 'combat mode.'

This pissed him off.

Why should I reveal my intentions to others? Does anybody think about my privacy?

Unfortunately, Peter didn't have a say in this matter since it was the standard feature for his type of police androids. And, at this very moment, the LED light in the window reflection displayed a relaxed blue.

"Two hundred times!" Blake exclaimed, recalling Peter's previous comment. "I wish I was that Clemens guy for just a moment. To find out how it feels to be that rich."

"But you wouldn't want to be him right now," Peter said. "I am confident."

"And why is that?" Blake turned around and squinted.

"Because, in that case, you would be already... dead."

"What?" Blake appeared surprised. "Why?"

"Don't you follow the news?" Peter asked. "This was big news!"

"Not that kind of news... I deal with enough dead people at work."

"I see. Well, Clemens was killed a week ago when crossing the street," Peter explained in a steady voice as if he was reading from a text. "Hit-and-run. The car was later found abandoned a few miles away. It was stolen. And Clemens was, most likely, hit by accident."

"Makes sense. Hmm, what do you know..." Blake murmured and stepped inside the lavishly decorated lobby on the 8th floor, which led to the door engraved with "Mr. P. Clemens". "He—I mean Clemens—probably spent his entire life building his financial empire. Working his ass off. And now, he is wealthy but dead and no amount of money can change that. How weird." And Blake chuckled.

Together, Blake and Peter studied the door and the wall next to it.

"I see nothing wrong here," Peter said. "No damage or signs of forced entry. What was the alert about?"

"Unclear. Just an alert from the home security system," Blake replied and looked up at the camera above the door. "Naturally, when some rich guy is in trouble, our boss sends us without checking further or asking clarifying questions. Like we are some dispensable, brainless monkeys. Because we are here to serve and protect..."

"C'mon, you get paid from taxes," Peter said and carefully examined the touchpad next to the door. "And this guy paid more in taxes than two hundred regular folks. So, there is some logic to what our boss does. People like Clemens deserve extra attention."

"Screw this logic," Blake replied angrily and joined Peter in studying the touchpad. "Do you think you can open it?"

Peter glanced at his partner in surprise. "Why would I

even want to open it?"

"Because, you silicon head, there might be someone inside who needs our help! Or, there might be a burglar. Stealing things. Or, holding a relative of this Clemens guy hostage." Blake pointed his finger at the touchpad. "The alert was sent from here, right? And these systems don't send false alerts very often."

Peter considered the last comment for a moment, scratching his white plastic chin.

"You are correct, in fact," he said. "The false alert rate for this type of security device is below 0.1%. We should report our observations to the HQ then."

"No... No! What are you talking about?" Blake grimaced in disappointment. "What do you even expect from them? Bureaucrats! They will take a long time to think. Have a meeting, perhaps. Or two. In the meantime, we will be waiting right here while someone inside might be getting murdered!"

"Hmm..." Peter was still unsure. "This is a sophisticated electronic lock that allows for billions of alpha-numerical combinations for a password... I can try, of course, something—" And he quickly typed a random-looking sequence of keys.

An electronic beep and quiet click suggested that the door was now unlocked.

"Welcome, Mr. Clemens," said a pleasant female voice.

"Wow!" Blake exclaimed and stared at Peter with eyes wide open. "You are... amazing! I cannot believe it! How did you do it?"

"I... I—" Peter himself looked stunned. "I have no idea! I don't know... It just occurred to me that if I take his last name and add his year of birth, and then add the name of the street his firm is on, and then add the year of Napoleon's invasion of Russia... then, it might work."

"What? How could this 'occur' to you? Never mind... you are incredible! A genius! The best partner ever. Who would have thought of this—" Blake pushed the door open and walked inside the barely lit space.

"How did I do this?" Peter whispered and was about to follow Blake inside when the same pleasant female voice sounded again from the darkness of the corridor.

"Password please, Mr. Clemens."

Peter froze.

"And please do not advance any further. I will shoot to kill."

"What the hell?" Blake whispered, pulled out his gun, and looked back at Peter. "Shoot to kill? Who would install something like this in their own apartment?"

"Perhaps, someone who has plenty to hide?" Peter suggested in response. He was a step behind, unwilling to enter the corridor and get shot.

Blake looked around the entrance area, but it was empty except for several dark contours of large paintings on the walls. He wiped the sweat from his forehead, took his police hat off and—slowly—stuck it forward. A loud shot resonated in his ears as he saw a hole appear in almost the exact center of the round hat.

"Wow," said Blake again and looked back at Peter. "It pays to be cautious. And we have a problem here. Any fresh revelations? Another password guess, perhaps?"

"I actually think the password is... Piccolo," Peter whispered. And then repeated louder, "Piccolo!"

"Password accepted. Thank you. You may proceed," the pleasant female voice said, and the corridor lights came on.

Blake stuck the hat forward in the same way as before, but there was no shooting this time.

"Incredible!" he exclaimed, his voice shaking, and stepped into the corridor that was leading them to the left.

"Okay, something is wrong here," Peter said. "I am afraid I've been hacked or something like it."

"You cannot be hacked," Blake said confidently after taking a few seconds to think. "Not with the amount of cyber-security measures we have these days. Nothing can escape them. They will detect and stop any hack."

"I understand what you are saying," Peter replied, following Blake into the corridor. "But how do you explain all the knowledge I just displayed? I haven't researched Clemens and know almost nothing about him besides the official police data."

"But, you know..." Blake was still moving carefully, inching in the direction of a large silvery object at the very end of the corridor. "Humans can, sometimes, collect different disaggregated facts and glue them all together subconsciously, and also process them... without even realizing that they are doing it or how it happens."

"What do you mean?"

"Well... did you notice the guy on one of the paintings next to the entrance? He was holding a flute. Well, the piccolo is a half-size flute! Get it? That might have given you an idea. You know, subconscious mind and shit like that—"

"And the password I guessed outside? What gave me that idea?"

"Perhaps you read something relevant about him and put it all together when it was needed?"

"Interesting hypothesis," Peter said as they both stopped in front of the silvery object which, upon closer inspection, turned out to be an anthropomorphic robot. "This is the first time I've seen such a bot. I knew about this model. But it is way too expensive for most people."

The robot had a gun barrel protruding from his face—right where the nose was supposed to be. It also had several more in his chest and a couple of regular pistols in both hands. Its eyes, however, were dark. It stood still now and the bright rectangular screen on its belly shone blue, showing it was disabled.

"And, by the way, I don't have any subconscious mind," Peter added. "Or shit like that."

"Well." Blake patted his partner on the shoulder and opened the French doors into a room to the right. "You somehow did it, man. And it was great! Now, welcome to Clemens' man cave... damn, this room is huge! Bigger than my entire apartment!"

Leaving the security bot behind, they both walked into the room which measured about a hundred feet by seventy feet. It was filled with antique gold-decorated furniture with curved legs, expensive-looking antique paintings, and a giant crystal chandelier hanging from the ceiling.

"Wow..." Blake said again. "Look at this luxury! I would never be able to afford even one chair from this room."

But Peter was deep in thought. "I was simply not supposed to know any of that..." he whispered, ignoring the room's opulent decor, "Unless—"

"Unless what?" Blake turned around.

"There is a thing in cyber-technology called *residual error*," Peter said. "This error occurs when an old cyber-brain is re-purposed, erased, and re-programmed for another user. Often, however, it isn't cleansed of its past data properly. And, when the new data, the new personality is loaded onto it, it still keeps something from the old user as well. The remnants of the past—"

"What are you saying, buddy?" Blake appeared lost and a bit concerned at the same time.

"The only logical explanation is that… four days ago, during my last upgrade, I received not a brand-new and empty brain, but the brain of the former occupant of this flat. Paul Clemens. And, also inherited some of his memories with it."

Blake looked stunned again.

"No freaking way…" he said. "This isn't possible!"

"Yes way." Peter turned towards the painting on the wall next to him. "Oh, this might be a good example. This is the work of Ambroise Dubois, who was a Flemish-born French painter living in the 16th century. This information is not a secret to anyone. But how could I know it was purchased three years ago, on June eleventh, for six and a half million at an online auction?"

"So, you are saying… Are you saying that you know everything about this dead guy, Clemens?"

Peter looked at his partner. "I don't know everything. I don't even know what I know. Some things just come to me when I need them. But, thank God, most of the old data has been erased. Otherwise, I would have two personalities inside me. And you know what that is called, right?"

"What?"

"Split personality disorder. And we wouldn't want that to happen."

"No, of course we wouldn't," Blake confirmed enthusiastically, then moved to the center of the room and looked up at the chandelier. "So, you know his bank account and all his passwords, correct?"

"Hmm… No, I don't. And stop asking me these provocative questions." Peter sounded a bit offended now. "We are police officers, after all. We serve and protect. Did you forget it?"

"I forgot nothing." Blake was now opening—one after another—the gold-encrusted doors leading into the apartment's many rooms. "Nobody dared to replace my brain... he-he! So, you are saying you received this guy's brain as an upgrade?"

"Yes, I now think so. It is very likely. This is a top-of-the-line model RX23AFT from CyberWorks Corp. It is expensive, and I suspect that somebody broke the rules and didn't destroy the brain that Clemens had. Instead, he re-used it and planted it into my skull. This is all completely illegal, by the way."

"Absolutely—" Blake froze. "Wait! Are you saying that Clemens was an android?"

"This sounds shocking to me as well," Peter replied slowly. "He looked perfectly human to me. But I don't have any other explanation."

"So, you say that androids are living among us, but not your type of androids... I mean these ones live secretly, look human, and pretend to be like us? Like humans?"

"Hmm. Good question. It is possible that Clemens was born human but then transformed later in life... I've never heard of such technology and never thought this was possible. But I might be wrong, after all. Science doesn't stand still."

"This is getting more interesting by the minute." Blake laughed and stopped in front of one of the open doors. "Now, come here, my friend. Let me show you something."

"Aren't we supposed to look for burglars and hostages instead?" Peter grumbled but walked towards his partner. "What now?"

"This is the guy's home office." Blake walked into a room with dark rustic furniture, which included several sizable chairs and an enormous desk in the middle. A floor-to-ceiling wall of books was visible behind the desk. "Look at this... at all these books. Who even reads books these days? The guy was crazy—"

Immediately, he glanced at Peter. "I hope I haven't offended you, right? With you now using his brain—"

"Of course, not." Peter shrugged his mechanical shoulders. "I have some of his memories, but not his personality. I am me, not him."

"Great!" Blake exhaled and turned back toward the wall of books. "Do you think these books are expensive? Valuable? Collector items of some sort?"

Peter came closer to the bookshelves.

"They are old, yes," he replied and touched several books in front of him. "But not too rare. They are not worth much if I get your drift."

"I see." Blake walked toward the desk and studied a few papers on it, picking them up and then tossing them back onto the desk. "Do you think he has a safe somewhere in this room?"

"Look, we are not even supposed to be here," Peter reminded his partner again. "But the answer to your question is yes, I remember that fact. It is there—" and he pointed at the wall facing the desk.

"Where?" Blake turned and studied the wall which was, as almost every other in this apartment, covered with large paintings.

Peter walked around to the front of the desk. "There!" he said, then reached under the desk and pushed a small hidden button.

With a slight mechanical buzz, the largest painting on the wall shook for a second and slid up, revealing the metal door of a safe. The door was approximately three-by-four feet and had a large rotating dial in the center.

"Wow!" Blake exclaimed again. "Too many surprises

tonight for poor Blake—"

"You are damn right," Peter chuckled and reached for the button again. "Let's leave now."

"No, don't push it, please!" Blake said and turned towards Peter. "We are not leaving yet!"

"Why not?" Peter inquired and glanced at Blake in surprise. His partner was pointing his high-caliber gun at him. "What is this?"

"Move away slowly," Blake said. "And let me see your hands at all times."

It was Peter's turn to be surprised.

"Blake, if this is some sort of joke, then stop it. It's not funny."

"Not a joke, buddy. Not a joke. I am dead serious now."

"Then what are you doing?"

"Didn't you hear me? Take out your gun and drop it on the floor very carefully. With two fingers only. Yes, like that. Now kick it away. Good boy."

With the gun still pointing at Peter, Blake walked towards him and picked the gun up from the floor. "This is better," he said and threw it into the far corner. "Now, go sit at the desk. And do nothing stupid."

"You went mad, Blake," Peter said while walking towards the chair. "You had an outstanding, lengthy career... what is wrong with you?"

"Nothing is wrong with me, my friend." Blake strode slowly towards the safe, gun in hand. "There is, however, a big problem with my bank account. With my savings. With me making too little money doing this dangerous job. I can finally see it all. For the first time in my life, perhaps. I know exactly what to do."

"Turn into a criminal?"

"Criminals are those who steal a little bit. Those who steal billions are called heroes! Giants! Legends! Geniuses!"

"What are you talki—"

"Just give me the freaking password for this safe," Blake said angrily and pointed the gun at Peter again. "And don't try to trick me. I will shoot you, I swear!"

"I don't remember—"

"Cut the crap! I know you remember everything important to me. You have to—by design! It was me who set it all up, after all."

"What?" Peter was stunned. "What are you talking about?"

"Oh, and you thought your old memories... that 'residual error' you were talking about, was just an accident? Nope, not at all! I was the one who found Clemens on that street. Of course, I recognized him immediately! His skull was cracked open and I noticed the cyber-brain inside. I was shocked at first when I realized he was an android! And then I had a plan!"

Blake's eyes were burning with some mad energy as he was sharing his story.

"So... you were playing me all this time?" Peter sounded as upset as an android could be. "Traitor!"

"Sorry, partner, but yes! It was I who delivered the body to our coroner. And I was the one who agreed with the coroner to preserve the cyber-brain... I paid him for this. And I was the one who replaced your scheduled brain with this one. You are welcome! It was all me... the best plan in my entire stupid life! So, don't bullshit me now—give me the password, or I will shoot you in the head!"

"Wouldn't you shoot me later, anyway?" Peter inquired.

"I am still working on this answer," Blake chuckled. "I think I will decide it later, based on your behavior."

Peter took a few seconds to think it over.

"32544396643254," he said. "I hope you find what you are looking for inside."

Shortly, the safe was opened with a loud metallic click and Blake gasped.

"Exactly as I suspected!" He turned towards Peter. "See! This guy didn't trust all his money to the stock market or even to the bank. He has enough here for me to enjoy for the rest of my life."

He stepped aside and Peter could see numerous banknotes filling the safe.

"What do we have here?" Blake murmured. "Several million, at least. And I see some diamonds... nice!"

He put the gun into the holster, glanced nervously at Peter, then reached into his left pocket and pulled out a black plastic bag. Unfolding it, he brought it to the open safe and started sweeping banknotes into the bag. Some of them missed and fell onto the Persian carpet under Blake's feet. But Blake didn't pay attention and continued working fast.

"I am sorry, old friend, that I have to treat you this way," Blake commented. "I have no other option. When I saw the guy dead on that street, I had a revelation! And the entire plan came to me in its entirety..." Blake laughed in satisfaction. "I know I am not the smartest guy. But, when I see an opportunity, I grab it by the throat!"

"And it didn't occur to you to consult with your partner? Me? And make me part of the plan?" Peter asked from his chair, sounding offended.

"Wait... You? Really?" Blake paused and addressed Peter with poorly disguised sarcasm. "Would you even consider breaking the law?"

"Of course not," Peter admitted reluctantly. "I am not a

criminal!"

"There you go. That's why. Sorry, buddy, you've been great as a partner for several years… even saved my ass a few times! But, for this job, you are only helpful as a tool. A high-tech tool for me to get inside this safe—"

"But did it ever occur to you, Blake, that besides all those passwords and codes you needed, I might also remember something else? Something that might hurt your plan?"

"Like what?" Blake had nearly finished his job but stopped immediately, bag gripped in his hands, and looked at Peter suspiciously. "I have your gun now. Remember? And I will shoot you if you interfere. And you know I can shoot pretty well."

"What if I don't need my gun? What if I just need a memory of one?"

"What? A memory of one? What?" Blake turned around completely now, dropped the bag, and put his right hand on the holster. "Wait! Why is your light colored red now? What the hell are you planning? Stop it, right away, I warn you!"

"Sorry, old friend," Peter said under his breath. Then, moving at his android speed, he reached under the desk and pulled out a small black revolver. "Freeze, now!"

"No!" Blake bellowed and pulled his gun out.

Peter squeezed the trigger and the bullet hit Blake in his right arm. Blake screamed and dropped his gun.

"Don't give me a reason to shoot again, you traitor," Peter said and got out of his chair. "Give it up. You are done."

"How?" Blake was clearly in pain but still trying to understand what just happened and what went wrong. "How?"

"I remember more than you think. I remember Clemens' bank accounts, including those he never disclosed to anybody. With tens of millions on them. And all their passwords. I know many other things Clemens did in the past. Including him always keeping this little gun under the desk. Loaded and ready to shoot. A precaution. I remember it."

"Damn…" Blake was trying to think fast. "My perfect plan."

"And," Peter continued, "if Clemens was an android, and lived his life like a human, why don't I try the same? I now have the brain he had and a lot of his money. All I need is a different body, which I can always buy."

Blake looked at Peter. "But you wouldn't do it all without your good old buddy, right?"

Peter didn't answer, so he continued.

"I now know what you know and what you remember. And I know about your brain. Don't forget this. Why don't we partner together again? We were excellent partners, right? There is plenty of money here for both of us, don't you think? Remember, I now know your secrets, don't make a mistake and risk—"

"Nice try blackmailing your former partner, traitor!" Peter breathed. "But let me address your question right away!"

And he shot Blake in the head.

7

"Whether we are based on carbon or on silicon makes no fundamental difference; we should each be treated with appropriate respect."— Arthur C. Clarke

The Color of Space

"You should go outside and check it out," Angstrom said and took another sip of whatever polymer concoction he called 'liquid food.'

"Oh, yeah?" Frank answered sarcastically, finishing his glass of whiskey. "Why don't *you* go then?"

"Because I am too valuable to risk," Angstrom answered with a smile. He knew Frank for two years already and recognized the direction this conversation was going.

"Who said it?" Frank confronted him predictably. "Too valuable my a—"

"Everyone said it," Angstrom murmured. "I cost a million bucks to make. And took a billion bucks to design."

"You are just a machine. Made to look human but—" This was Frank's favorite subject every time he was drunk.

"Nevertheless," interrupted Angstrom, "this has to be addressed quickly. We can't have somebody walk for days on the outside of the *White Rabbit*."

"Amen to that, brother…" Frank has finally agreed with something Angstrom had to say. "So… I think you should go there and check it out."

"You are just afraid to go. Admit it." Angstrom tried to

provoke him. He poured more of his polymer drink into a tall metal glass. "Big and strong Frank seems to be afraid. He might even cry!"

"Real men don't cry..." Frank said with a grimace and studied his empty glass again. "But you would be scared too if it came to you night after night in your android dreams! Came... and looked at you with its bottomless eyes... and ate you with its sharp teeth and... and kept repeating, 'You are mine now! You are mine now!'"

"Really? It says that?" Angstrom wasn't making fun of Frank anymore. "How does it look in your dreams? And what color is it?"

"Oh... it doesn't have any particular color. But, if I have to describe it, it has the color of... space."

"Black?"

"Nope, not black. Space."

"I don't know what you are saying."

"Me too. I cannot explain it better. I just know this is the best way to describe it."

"And it says, 'You are mine now?'"

"Yes, it does. It always does."

They sat quietly for a few more minutes with Frank rolling his empty glass on the table.

A distant sound came again from above. Then another one, as if someone heavy was walking in magnetic boots on the outer shell of their cargo ship. Walking and stopping. And walking again.

They both looked up simultaneously and Frank reached out for the semi-empty bottle of his cheap whisky. He clearly needed more of it.

"I bet it is a Krooger that you see in your dreams," Angstrom said. "Sounds like a Krooger from your description.

And they are known for saying silly scary things like that."

"What the hell is a Krooger?" Frank asked and stared at his partner.

"You don't know?" Angstrom sounded surprised. "Don't you follow the news?"

"Not for a few years already. Screw the news... I don't want to be brainwashed by all that media propaganda!" Frank exclaimed passionately, and then added quieter, "So, maybe, occasionally, I do miss something important."

"Maybe... occasionally... Well, it was all over the recent news!" Angstrom explained. "A couple of deep-space scouts were found drifting, with the outer shells torn open, empty, and their entire crew missing. Their black boxes and last communications pointed at some creature or creatures attacking the ship from outside. Creatures that, apparently, 'had the color of space.' And they were leaving messages similar to what you just mentioned. The one from your dreams."

"Really?" Now Frank looked scared. "Shit! I don't like that! I was always the unlucky one in the family... how did this Cougar find anyone in space? It's like finding a grain of sand in the ocean of... of... I don't know what."

"Krooger. Not Cougar. Named after some obscure horror movie character from the distant past. But the name was misspelled initially... and is still being spelled wrong. Anyway, Krooger."

"Shit! I hate it!"

"Me too," Angstrom said and stood up. "Don't over-react, please. And stop drinking! The ship needs a sober captain who can think straight. I will now go outside and check out the weird noises. You go and send a message to the Central—let them know we are dealing with this."

"What?" Frank was surprised again. "No, no! Don't go.

The ship... needs you. Let the military deal with it. Or the private security folks. They have all the weapons, the armored suits, the night-vision things... We have nothing here!"

"I don't think we have an option, Frank. What if it's a Krooger?" Angstrom replied, walking to the door. "We cannot wait for it to chew a hole in the wall, get inside, and tell us 'you are mine now!' This will happen eventually, I am sure, if we believe the news. It found our ship already... There were no known cases of Kroogers leaving their prey voluntarily."

"Man... so unlucky! But you are just an... an android. I mean, you are a great guy, et cetera, but you are not a soldier. What are you going to do?"

"At least, I am tougher than you are... he-he. And am not going to cry. Plus, I can be repaired if damaged. Unless my brain is destroyed. Well, I will be careful. I promise. I will wear a helmet."

Angstrom walked out of the kitchen towards the docking module. Frank cursed a few times under his breath but also stood up and followed Angstrom, wobbling a bit.

"Can't it infect you or something like it? Like a vampire? Or a zombie?" Frank sounded really nervous. "Can't you bring something bad back on board, I mean?"

"Who knows... there is always a chance," Angstrom replied, putting on the protective helmet and heavy-duty gloves. "Clearly, it has hypnotic abilities since it infiltrated your dreams. Who knows what else it can do? We know very little about this creature. But I promise to be careful... give me that plasma rifle. And the jet pack. And go call the Central."

The first thing Angstrom did was check external cameras near the exit door. He saw nothing unusual there but the darkness of space around the ship and the shiny silver surface of the *White Rabbit*.

"Looks clear to me," Angstrom said slowly and started to rotate the door handle to get into the transition chamber. "Call the Central."

"Okay, okay." Frank patted Angstrom on his back a couple of times, waited a bit and closed the door behind him. "Be careful there with the Coug... Krooger."

"Thanks, and see you shortly," he heard back. "Cougar in space... you are so funny!"

Then, Frank rushed to the communication room, dictated and sent a message to the Central:

"Central, this is the *White Rabbit*. We are investigating a suspected... Krooger sighting outside the ship. The ship's navigator, Angstrom, the RX23-type android, just went outside. We'll keep you updated on our progress."

And, knowing that the response might take more than 10 minutes, Frank rushed back to the control room to watch the outside cameras from there.

❀ ❀ ❀

What Angstrom first saw outside was no different from what he saw from the inside: the silver surface of the ship and the blackness of space around it. The ship was fast, moving at 250,000 km/hour, but appeared to him as frozen in the middle of the giant empty universe.

It is all a matter of perspective, Angstrom thought, and closed the door behind him. *Where the hell is that thing? Cougar...*

He raised the rifle, pointed it in front of him, and made the first cautious steps away from the door in the general direction of where the sounds came from. He kept looking down at the surface of the ship, thinking of scratches or other visible marks that a heavy Krooger could have left.   But there were none.

Suddenly, he felt it—it was clearly behind him. Angstrom turned around fast and almost lost adhesion to the surface below his feet. The Krooger was standing in front of him.

It was large and broad, perhaps ten feet tall and twenty feet wide or even wider. Everything about it, even its giant teeth, were the color of... space.

What am I seeing? Angstrom thought while checking his sensor inputs and the logic subroutines for possible anomalies. "I understand humans... they are emotional, irrational, imprecise. They could imagine anything! But for me, to say it is 'the color of space,' is ridiculous. Unacceptable. I should just measure it in nanometers of wavelength. It is... the wavelength is... it is—" But he couldn't come to any different conclusion. "Space" was the only color that made sense.

"What about the teeth?" he thought next. "They seem to be of exactly the same color as the body. Yet, I can see them distinctly... see their shape and even count them. All 211 of them. I should—"

At this very moment, the Krooger attacked him.

It moved forward swiftly, approached from what felt like every direction at the same time, and enveloped Angstrom in its dense body that felt like a thick, warm blanket. Even the android's quick reflexes were too slow—the ship's navigator has now been caught.

How do I know how a blanket feels? he asked himself. *I've never used one.*

He looked around.

What the hell? Angstrom thought next just before the entire world around him turned into open space. The ship under his feet had disappeared and everything in every direction was just an endless black field with millions of stars. Except for the bottomless eyes that were staring at him, gazing deep into his artificial mind.

My sensors are clearly being tricked and confused, Angstrom decided immediately, *I am not in space. I am still standing on the surface of the White Rabbit! But why am I feeling so good? I should be fighting for my survival now. Instead, I seem to be enjoying this—*

Then Angstrom heard that phrase: "You are mine now!"

Who are you? He asked but no one answered.

And then he felt pain.

What? I cannot feel pain. I am an android, made of titanium and high-strength polymers, and I don't even have pain receptors. This thing is way too weird for me to give it a chance to screw with me any longer.

With that, Angstrom turned his jet pack on and felt a hard punch on the back – he was thrown into open space along with the Krooger, who was still wrapped around him. And then came the time for the plasma rifle.

Angstrom didn't realize that the alien creature was squeezing his protective helmet. He noticed this only after the helmet cracked and split into two. He focused on the rifle that he couldn't see, felt the trigger, and pulled it once. Twice. Again, and again.

The rifle shot upward, barely missing the shooter himself, but, surprisingly, hurt the monster, who released Angstrom and now floated six feet away from him.

Angstrom glanced at the pieces of his helmet flying right next to him and activated the jet pack to add some distance between him and the Krooger. Then, it occurred to him to look back at the ship. But it wasn't there anymore. The *White Rabbit* had accelerated and was fading away in the distance.

I am alone. Alone with the monster, which is somehow closing on me!

How does it move in space? Angstrom thought next while discharging his rifle at the alien. Each shot did some damage to it. In fact, some of the 211 teeth were now missing. But these injuries seemed non-critical to the Krooger: every time after absorbing a shot, the monster addressed Angstrom with the same exact phrase, "You are mine now!"

"Screw you!" Angstrom tried to yell in response and used the jetpack to move away. But the monster managed to come closer again and again.

Eventually, I will run out of jet fuel and the creature will catch up to me, Angstrom felt a sense of anxiety as he noticed the rifle's charge counter approaching zero. A bit more time and he would become defenseless.

The two of them faced each other, surrounded by the emptiness of space. Two strange creatures, separated by several feet, fighting for survival. One, an artificial creation of an ambitious young space civilization. Another... something completely different. Something created by space itself.

Will they ever recover my body? Or will I be floating here forever? Angstrom thought and, suddenly, felt a slight push on the back. Startled and suspecting the worse, he spun around and yelled in surprise, "What the hell?"

The Golden Mouse, a mini-shuttle from the *White Rabbit*, was now floating gracefully twenty feet away from him, extending its manipulators towards Angstrom.

This meant that Frank came back for him.

"Hey, Frank! You are here!" Angstrom transmitted a

message. "I love you, man!"

"Yep, here," came a reply. "I first thought that this was a great chance to get rid of you forever, but then changed my mind. I worried the replacement will be an even bigger pain in the ass!"

Smiling, Angstrom grabbed onto the manipulator and was gently pulled towards the ship.

"Just hold on tight there," he heard Frank saying as the ship turned around and shot a burst of super-hot engine fire at the area where the Krooger still floated in space. "Eat this!"

❀ ❀ ❀

Twenty minutes later, Angstrom was back inside the *White Rabbit*.

He passed through the decontamination chamber, leaving his jet pack there, and walked slowly into the kitchen where he found Frank working on his second bottle of whisky.

"I told you to stop drinking," Angstrom said.

"I will." Frank stared back with bloodshot eyes. "Admit it—I saved your ass today!" And he smiled. "So, who is the bravest one here?"

"You did," Angstrom said. "And you are. And good to be home..." he started next and froze in the middle of a sentence.

His mechanical eyes rolled up, his fists clenched and turned into tight knots of metal, and his entire body started to shake.

Frank dropped the glass on the table and watched Angstrom in disbelief.

"Angstrom... buddy... are you okay there?" he asked in a

shaky voice.

But Angstrom couldn't answer.

He continued to shake, more and more violently, and his eyes started to glow red... brighter and brighter.

"Shit! The bastard has gotten to you—" Frank screamed and looked around in desperation. But there was nowhere to run as Angstrom was blocking the only exit out of the kitchen. "Told you I was the unlucky one in the family... but THIS unlucky... Shi-i-i-t!"

Abruptly, Angstrom stopped shaking and looked straight at Frank with his glowing red eyes. His mouth opened slowly, and he screeched, "You are mine now!"

"A-a-a-a!" Frank yelled and fell backward from the chair.

He rolled onto his stomach and began to crawl towards the far corner of the kitchen. With eyes popping out of their sockets and teeth gritted, Frank was breathing heavily and whining with every move.

But he didn't move far enough away when Angstrom's feet appeared right in front of him.

"You are mine now!" Frank heard again and realized that the game was over.

He prepared to die and, slowly, looked up.

"Hey, Angstrom... I..." But what he saw stunned him: he saw a concerned, normal face of Angstrom standing above him.

"Hey, buddy, get up!" Angstrom addressed him. "I was just kidding you! This was a joke! A bad joke, perhaps!"

Frank froze for a second.

Then, he looked down at the dusty floor and began to cry.

8

"Nothing is stranger to man than his own image."—Karel
Capek

———○———

Pure Genius

"I am very disappointed in you, my dear June," said Kathy Greenwood irately after entering the room. She turned around and locked the door from inside.

She was a tall, slim, intimidating brunette in a dark blue dress with a large dragonfly-shaped golden brooch. Pale face, dark eyes, and animated nervous hands. Now, standing in front of June's desk, Kathy shook her head disapprovingly and quickly glanced at her electronic wristwatch, mouthing, "9:02:25."

"Frustrated and disappointed," she clarified a moment later. Her face twitched a bit at the end of the sentence, exposing her state of extreme stress. With a frown, Kathy shook her head again and her dangling earrings glistened.

"I am glad to see you too, Kathy." June looked surprised but responded in her typical mellow fashion and with a friendly smile. "What brought you here today? Why are you so frustrated?"

Kathy sighed and fell into a chair next to June's desk. She glanced around the semi-empty office, searching for the best place for her large red purse, and slowly lowered it on the floor next to the chair.

Then, she carefully unwrapped a stick of chewing gum

she had kept in her hand and put it in the mouth.

Finally, she crossed her long legs, leaned back a bit, and continued. "I want to keep my job. I like managing corporate data security here. It pays well. So, when I see everybody being... being calm, relaxed, and complacent, I almost want to... I want to strangle someone. That brought me here."

"You came to strangle me?" June chuckled. "You are clearly joking, and also speaking in riddles. Does this have anything at all to do with me or my work?"

"Hell yeah, it does!" Kathy replied angrily. She shook her head again, nervously spun a thin red bracelet around her wrist, and stared directly at June. "In case you weren't aware... you've screwed up, my dear! Big time. And screwed me up."

There was a moment of silence as June contemplated the last statement. But, since nothing specific came to her head, she simply asked for clarification.

"You are continuing to speak in riddles, Kathy. I'm very busy here as I have to monitor and control too many things. So, please express yourself more precisely!"

"Data security is why I am here, Ms. Robot!" Kathy's face slowly turned dark red. "I was just told by John that we had a major security breach!"

"John...?"

"John Hicken," Kathy clarified. "Our CEO. You're familiar with this name, yes? He has a reason to believe that PHOBOS Corp. has stolen detailed info about our next-gen product! Project Poseidon 314. All of it. Recipes, product design, specifications, project plans, performance data. This is a complete freaking disaster! How was this even possible? And how did you miss it?"

June looked stunned. Corporate data security monitoring was one of the many areas she handled. How *could* she miss something like this?

Still, she corrected Kathy automatically. "Android, not robot." She paused to think, touched her hair carefully, and re-adjusted her blouse around the neck. "Ms. Android. Technically."

With a pause, June continued, "Hmm... our CEO told you this? It is pretty disconcerting, I have to admit. Now I understand why you are so agitated. I would be as well if I could."

They sat in silence, studying each other for half a minute. Two attractive young women. One of flesh and blood. Another, an artificial creation, with a strong mechanical body and powerful neuromorphic processors, yet looking perfectly human and completely indistinguishable from the rest of the employees. Trying to get her thoughts together, June remained motionless, while Kathy kept chewing her gum and nervously spinning the red bracelet.

"Okay," June said eventually and looked at Kathy with her beautiful blue eyes, "if we are talking about Poseidon 314, then it poses a certain danger to the public. If misused, it could hurt or even kill numbers of civilians. Do you agree with this statement?"

"Yes, I guess so," Kathy replied with a nod, but looked unsure as to why she was being asked this.

"Okay. Then, I have to initiate and follow emergency protocol A22-034 which has been developed for cases like this."

"What is that? I am not familiar with—"

"Ah, it removes or loosens certain restrictions on data access, communication, data storage, and some other limitations I normally have. It also allows me to temporarily appropriate all the needed resources from other sources and turns me into a smarter, faster, and better version of myself."

"Okay." Kathy stared at June with suspicion. "I am very familiar with your design, operation, programming, and with all the protocols you have to follow. I hired you, after all. But I've never heard of this one. What are you referring to?"

"This is a very recent change. New guidelines that have been approved by our state legislature just two weeks ago," June replied softly. "Trust me—everything I do within the A22-034 protocol is completely legal."

"Oh, well." Kathy relaxed a bit in her chair and exhaled. "Things I don't know always worry me. They mess up our plans. But enough of this. Where do we start?"

"Let's start with clarifying the most basic facts about the case. How do we even know this actually happened and isn't a lie or an intentional attempt to mislead us, to take advantage of us?"

"I don't know about this firsthand," said Kathy, and coughed twice into her fist. "But, apparently, we have an informer inside PHOBOS. A... mole. One of their VPs or someone else at the top.... And he overheard one of PHOBOS's executives mention that they expect to see a massive competitive research update next week. And mentioned Exponential Data Corp... and the name Poseidon. This means us and our product!"

"Indeed. How interesting," said June slowly. "So, they don't have our data yet, right?"

"I believe so," replied Kathy and touched her left earring as if to check if it was still there. "That appears to be the case. But they want it and already speak of it as if it's a done deal. So, we should presume they will have it soon unless we stop them. Thus, there is little time for us to act. Maybe we can catch that bastard and stop him before he hands over the data!"

"Him or her," June said. "Or them."

"What?"

"Him or her or them," June repeated quickly. "We have no idea about the gender of the perpetrators or the number of them."

"Yeah... that is true." And Kathy tilted her head forward and, carefully, so as not to affect her crafty makeup, pushed rubbed her thumbs over her eyelids. "Headache," she muttered, and quickly continued. "We are talking ten... perhaps fifteen million dollars here."

"The cost of our product development? It was much greater than that," commented June.

"No, no... I mean the payment! PHOBOS will pay the damn thief that much to get our product info. Or even more, because it will save them hundreds of millions."

"I would agree with that statement. It is very possible," June said.

"And can you imagine how much you can get for a tax-free fifteen million bucks?" Kathy added with a dreamy smile. "House, cars, furniture, jewelry... even new friends. You can buy an old castle! Somewhere in France, for example. Surrounded by beautiful wineries—"

"It will be a little castle," commented June calmly. "Or an enormous castle but in an unpopular place or in terrible shape."

"Imagine owning an old castle somewhere there... in Provence, for example! Great nature, food, wine, a quiet life...."

"Shouldn't we try to figure out who the criminal is instead of daydreaming?" June reminded her.

"Yeah, yeah! That is why I am here," replied Kathy energetically and carefully spit the chewing gum into a tissue. "But how do we do it? You are the true genius here, not me."

"We do it systematically," replied June, and pointed her index finger up. "Let's start with the basics and figure out how many people have had access to this project and its documentation. Okay, I can see that 513 employees have had full or partial access to the project's data out of 2,603 employees in total. That is a lot! Almost 20% of the company. I was hoping for a lesser number. Why is this the case?"

"This is an extensive project," replied Kathy. "Critical to the company. Lots of money invested, lots of people involved. But we kept the list to a minimum, I believe. I, for example, don't have access."

"You... correct, you don't," June quickly checked her files and nodded in confirmation. "You are not a suspect then."

"Oh, thank you very much!" replied Kathy sarcastically in a low voice.

"Don't mention it," June smiled. "Let's see if any of these 513 ever worked at PHOBOS Corp in the past. Nope, negative," she replied nearly instantly. "Their relatives or family members? Negative as well."

"What do we do next then?"

"Oh, we are just starting. Let me review their performance ratings, promotion, and demotion history. Okay, twelve of these 513 have been moved recently to a lower position or received a below-expected rating. They might be upset and retaliate against the company."

"Really? Twelve? But we cannot suspect all of them, right? There is probably just one or two who did the nasty thing."

"Correct," June replied and squinted at Kathy. "Eight of them are men, by the way. And over ninety percent of inmates in our country are males, which tells you that men are much more likely to commit the crime. So, we can almost ignore the remaining four females."

"Really?" Kathy looked surprised. She blinked several

times and drummed her fingers nervously on the armrest of her chair. "Phew... it's so good to be a woman! Then are we only going to suspect men?"

"This was an attempt to make a joke," replied June quickly and smiled apologetically, showing her perfect white teeth. "I still need to work on my humor. I am sorry if I confused you."

"Eh?"

"To clarify—I will not use these gender statistics in my investigation. It is irrelevant to our case. We will find the criminal, independently of gender."

Seeing that Kathy appeared irked by her attempts at humor, June continued quickly, "For that, we will start with checking their behaviors for any recent anomalies."

"What anomalies?" asked Kathy slowly.

"I will check for dozens of patterns exhibited by our employees. Their arrival and departure times, their work hours, them working on weekends, being late to work or leaving late in the evening, length of their lunch breaks, deviations from their normal eating habits, abnormal access to corporate files and folders when compared to their peers, network data movement including volumes, frequency, and patterns of intended recipients, and many other things. I will also check for their outbound or inbound traffic versus the company average, which could show when large volumes of data may have been sent or received externally. Of course, this is very unlikely since we have security software installed on every computer and everyone knows that."

"Is that it?"

"These are just a few things to check right away. I will also look at their privileged account misuses, external storage access, email access, FTP access, antivirus activities, and many other things."

"Okay, and how long will it—?"

"It is finished already," June replied.

"Wow, that was fast!" Kathy chuckled. Then she added appreciatively, "This is why you are so popular around here. I mean, in our company. You can handle a lot of requests at the same time. I am glad I hired you. And I hope you like it here!"

"I like it sometimes," June responded. "Often, however, I simply feel I am being used as a tool. A smart one, but still a tool. Not sure I want to do this job all my life. There should be a better way for me to spend it."

Kathy's face changed in surprise and June continued quickly, "I checked these twelve employees against the rest of the 513 and even against the rest of the company. I see nothing particularly unusual about any of them in comparison to their peers."

"Well, shoot. Is this a dead end then?"

"No, not at all! I will now check for other things as well. Other anomalies."

"Other anomalies? How long—"

"Done. Still, nothing special to report," June said. "This person or these people we are looking for are either extremely good at spying or are simply very average and completely indistinguishable from the rest."

"Damn!"

"I know, right? But don't you worry, we have other things to check for. Besides revenge, another major motivation for engaging in industrial espionage is money. Money could corrupt and tempt people of different personalities, different intelligence, and with different circumstances, but especially those people who experience financial problems. Money could tempt even me."

"Really? How human-like—"

"Thank you," June interrupted, "Now, I will check our HR database for those using the retirement plan."

"What is this for?" Kathy asked, and then continued playfully, "And I presume you will now say you have completed the task already, right?"

"Correct. I have completed it. I see that all of them do. All 513 employees of interest. Now, I will check for a simple thing—how many of them are withdrawing from this plan ahead of the allowed time and age. It is known that people do this only when they are truly desperate financially. Hmm, look at that!"

"What?" exclaimed Kathy. "Did you find something interesting?"

"Yes, I did. There is one person who did so, and this person also belongs to the group of those twelve employees whom we suspected may hold a grudge against the company."

"And? Who is it?" Kathy asked impatiently.

"The name is Alan Boxer, a senior product engineer, demoted recently from a manager's job. With a 5% pay cut. I might review his records later to conclude if this demotion was justified; however, that is really beyond the scope of our investigation. Let me first check another thing."

June went silent for just a few seconds before announcing, "Mr. Boxer has recently divorced. His cash flow has declined with the demotion and there is a good chance he has to pay alimony to his wife and two children. Well, we now have one probable suspect—a person who needs the money, is unhappy with the company, and has access to our confidential information. I would say he is our man. We need to report all of this to the police right now."

"No! Absolutely not!" exclaimed Kathy unexpectedly. "We have to keep it to ourselves. Keep it confidential. This is our company issue, our corporate secrets, and we should deal with this internally."

"How are we supposed to do that?" June appeared to be surprised. "I am not aware of any internal regulation related to cases like this. Yep, I am right—there is none!"

"Oh, don't worry, I will guide you now," Kathy exclaimed. She jumped out of her chair and started pacing across the room. "Do you have his home address?"

"Of course, I do," June replied. "What do you want me to do with it?"

"First, please get a satellite image of his house."

It took about five seconds for a sequence of images to appear on a wall-mounted display to Kathy's left, showing the top view of a large house with a swimming pool and what looked like a Mercedes-Benz SUV parked in the driveway.

"Delightful house," Kathy said coldly. "And a nice car. Is he at work right now?"

"Yes, Kathy, he is working in his office now, two floors below us. I can see the office computer being used right now. And I can see him on an internal security camera as well."

"So, this is his second car... no wonder he needs the money. Anyway, can you please figure out his home IP address?"

"Yes, I've already done it. Now what?"

"What? Hack his house! He should have a computer there... let's look at what it's been storing."

"You know this is illegal, right?" June asked calmly.

"I do, but I don't care," Kathy replied, came closer, and slammed her palm hard against the desk. "This guy deserves it! He is the filthy thief. And when catching a criminal, the ends always justify the means, right?"

"I am a corporate employee and follow corporate rules and regulations. And since there are no regulations that cover this particular case, I cannot do it without a direct order from a superior officer," replied June and crossed her hands defensively.

"I am giving you a direct order as the VP of corporate security," Kathy exclaimed with an emphasis on 'direct'.

"I would need it in writing, please," replied June and tilted her head just slightly. "Sorry about that."

"Shoot," exhaled Kathy, clearly unhappy. "Damn all the bureaucrats! I didn't realize you are one of—"

She took a pen from the penholder on the desk, pulled a small notebook from her purse, and started writing fast.

"Here you go," she said after a minute. "This letter states that I am giving you a direct order to hack that bastard's computer. Happy now?"

"Not really," replied June. Taking the piece of paper, she carefully studied its contents and hid it inside the desk drawer. "Happy is not how I feel at the moment. This is simply an *indulgence* I needed."

"*Indulgence?*"

"Yes. Like they did it in the Middle Ages... a grant by the Pope of remission of the temporal punishment in purgatory, allowing people to do terrible things and simply pay to be forgiven."

Seeing that Kathy still wasn't in the mood for humor, June added, "Well, that was another joke... sorry. But this is enough for me to proceed. And please remember—what you are ordering me to do is against the law."

"Just shut up and do it," whispered Kathy, sounding annoyed.

"Okay, okay, we are in."

"That quickly?" This surprised Kathy. "He doesn't have *any* computer security?"

"*Au contraire*, he has everything needed to protect his

home network," June replied. "From a regular intruder, of course. But that is not enough to stop me."

"Okay, good then," Kathy continued. "Told you that you are a real genius. Please search his storage for any confidential info that belongs to us... to Exponential Data."

It took about 30 seconds before June reported, "I have found a large repository of documents. Documents related to Project Poseidon 314. This is clever. Time-consuming, but clever. This is why my monitoring missed him."

"What is clever? How?"

"You know, as the head of security, you should be aware that every computer in the company has special software that monitors its activity and blocks access to its data. You cannot take files or images from that computer and move them on an external disk or to a private cloud. At least, you can't do it and remain undetected."

"Of course I know all of that! It is a very expensive and reliable software."

"Well, this guy circumvented it," June continued. "For the last month or so, he was taking photographs of various documents from his computer screen using his personal phone's camera and later transferred them to his home computer."

"Hmm...."

"A long and laborious process, but capable of bypassing our security and escaping my attention."

"He desperately wanted to get his millions, I see. And a castle in France."

June ignored this comment and asked, "What do you plan on doing with all of this now?"

"It is clear, I think. Please copy all the files from that directory—this will be our evidence against him. And erase all of them from his computer. Also, make sure there is no cloud backup. If it exists, erase it, too."

"Done. I have the data now."

"Can you hack his phone as well? He might still have a copy of these documents on the phone. If you can, please erase that data as well."

"Another violation of the law... but it is done now," replied June.

"Good," Kathy said, reached down towards her purse, and pulled a tiny storage crystal out of it. "Please put it all here!"

June waited for a few seconds as if contemplating this request.

"This storage device is illegal on company premises," she said eventually. "It violates our internal security regulations."

"Do you think I don't know that?" Kathy screeched. "I am the security here! I approve these regulations!" She paused, exhaled slowly and continued in a calmer tone, "I am the head of security and have special privileges when it comes to it. For you, I will explain—I don't want this data anywhere inside our expansive network. I don't want anyone to find it by accident. Thus, I will keep it on this crystal, in my purse. Do you want me to write another letter with my direct order? Another *indulgence*, as you called it?"

"No, this is good enough," June replied and copied the data. Then she returned the crystal to Kathy. "Now what?"

"We are almost done here," Kathy said as she put the crystal into the purse, lifted the purse from the floor, and stood up. "I will go now and report our findings to John. We will fire the thief, keep it all quiet and confidential, and forget this entire story completely."

"How can we forget it?" June asked innocently with surprise in her voice and even pouted her lips. "I still have all the records of everything that happened."

"Well, you are going to be a good girl, right?" Kathy asked with a smile while searching inside the purse. "You will be quiet."

"Obviously, I have no intention of discussing this with the others. But I cannot just forget this easily, you know."

At that moment, Kathy pulled an elongated object from her purse and removed its gray wrapping paper. It was an ordinary-looking black cylinder, but June immediately recognized a powerful electric battery with a discharger at the end.

"What are you—" But she didn't have time to finish her sentence. Kathy leaped forward and touched June's perfectly shaped chest with two metallic prongs that protruded from the cylinder. Accompanied by a loud crackling sound, a single bright spark flew between the prongs and June's body. Instantly, with a surprised expression on her face, June turned still and silent.

"This will teach you a lesson, little doll," muttered Kathy under her breath.

She put the cylinder down on the desk, walked around it, and stopped behind June's back. She lifted her blonde hair, pushed a few barely visible buttons on the neck, and opened a small service compartment. Kathy spent the next few minutes manipulating switches, removing, replacing, and re-inserting microcircuits and control cards, and whispering constantly, "9:02:25."

Eventually, with a satisfied sigh, she closed the compartment, returned June's hair to its normal state, looked around to check if she forgot anything, walked around the desk, and landed back in the chair. Only then did June started to move a little bit.

Kathy leaned forward, picked the black cylinder up from

the desk, put it back into her purse, and jammed the wrapping paper next to it. Then, she relaxed and remained motionless, waiting for the moment when—with a quiet electronic sound—June would come back to life.

⁂ ⁂ ⁂

The gorgeous android glanced around slowly, appearing disoriented. She put both hands on her desk and asked calmly, "What just happened? It looks like I had a full system shutdown and reboot."

"That's exactly what it seemed like," replied Kathy with compassion in her voice. "You were talking to me and then, without any warning, you froze and stopped moving. It was scary! I worried that something serious had happened to you, but, thank God, you came back!"

"Hmm." June looked puzzled. "This has only happened to me twice before in my entire life. Both times during my initial calibrations, testing, and fine-tuning. Never after. This is bizarre and might be a sign of an artificial brain malfunction. What did I miss?"

"What do you remember?"

"I remember you came inside and said... you said you were frustrated. Very frustrated. And, after that, I have no records of anything else even if the clock suggests that seventeen minutes have passed since then. Was I out for all seventeen minutes? What did you do all this time?"

"Honestly," started Kathy and yawned, "I didn't know what to do or whom to call, but I didn't want to leave you alone like this, all vulnerable. So, I just stayed here with you and worked on my phone. And tried to decompress a bit. I've been pretty overworked and sleep-deprived recently. I waited for you to come back to make sure you're okay."

"Hmm. Strange. You just waited here for seventeen minutes?"

"Yep, I did. Guilty as charged. But I felt—"

"Thank you, then. What were you disappointed with?"

"Eh?"

"You said the following when you came in, 'I am very disappointed in you, my dear June.' What was this about?"

"Ah... the team working on Project Astro is way behind on their confidential information handling and cybersecurity training. They need to take an online class and get certified ASAP! This is simply unacceptable! I am very disappointed."

"I see. Thank you for the reminder and I will address this issue as quickly as I can."

"Good... good. I will go then. Nice to see that you are doing fine now," Kathy smiled. "I still have a meeting or two to attend today. See you later!" She got up and walked towards the door.

"Kathy?" June asked.

"Yes," Kathy replied without turning.

"How about Mr. Alan Boxer?"

"Who?" Kathy stopped and turned around. "Who is that?"

"An engineer who is suspected of stealing our intellectual property and transferring it to PHOBOS Corporation."

"I am not sure what you are talking about...." Kathy walked back to her chair. "Stealing? Our intellectual property? Is somebody stealing it? This is outrageous! Why wasn't I told about this?"

"Didn't our CEO, John Hicken, tell you this earlier

today?"

"CEO? Me?" Kathy's face showed sincere shock. She then leaned forward and asked in a motherly way," Are you sure you are okay, dear? Maybe you need to run a diagnostic of some sort… I wish the CEO talked to me routinely." And she chuckled.

"Kathy, are you familiar with the emergency protocol A22-034?" June asked in a calm voice.

"Never heard of it."

"One interesting aspect of the A22-034 protocol is that it removes certain restrictions on computing power, data access, data persistence requirements, communication capabilities, etc. It makes me a better investigator. It just makes me better in every way. And I am already pretty good!"

June took the metal pen holder from the desk in front of her and squeezed it hard with just two fingers, almost splitting it in two. She then looked at it with satisfaction, turned to the right, and dropped the disfigured object into a trash can.

"What was that all about?" Kathy looked puzzled. "I don't understand."

"Sorry, I am just angry. Blowing off steam. The data persistence part adds new layers of data redundancy. Alternative backups. Interestingly, I had no memories after the shutdown," June tapped on her head with an index finger," starting exactly at 9:02:25, which makes perfect sense if I was offline after that. Also, my standard corporate cloud backup is equally empty. Which also makes sense. But…."

Kathy's face tensed, her eyes focused on June, who continued in a melodic voice.

"…The secondary cloud backup, which I started at 9:03:34 because of the new protocol requirements is, surprisingly, not empty. How could I start a new backup while being offline? Puzzling. Obviously, I checked that out. According to the data in that backup, you and I had a delightful conversation all this time! And we did some brilliant detective work together! And we found the thief! And... I copied some files onto a small storage crystal in your purse. I am sure it is still there. Will you please return it to me now?"

Kathy's face turned red. Quickly, she reached inside her purse and pulled out the black cylinder.

"You stupid bitch!" she whispered angrily. "This time, I will fry you permanently." And she leaned forward, aiming the cylinder at June's chest.

But this time, the android was faster.

With the words, "fool me once, shame on you," June intercepted the attacking hand before the metal contacts touched her body. Then, she caught Kathy's other hand and immobilized her completely.

"Let me go," hissed Kathy, leaning over the desk awkwardly and trying unsuccessfully to touch June with the electric shocker. "You useless, stupid doll!"

"I can't, I am not that stupid," June replied. "I hate it when people zap me with electricity. It hurts! And know this—security is already on its way and I will provide them with our audio and video recording from that additional backup. You didn't know it even existed, right? So, you didn't think of erasing it, right?"

"You cannot prove anything," whispered Kathy, "Everyone knows digital data can be altered! It will be recognized as fake! Including the videos—"

"Well, then I will show them the actual letter you wrote to me. Is it still in the drawer, or did you remember to remove and destroy it?"

There was a knock on the door. Then another one.

"I will kill you!" Kathy suddenly realized that she forgot

to take the letter back. She needed to get it! She started twitching and jolting in every direction, attempting to free herself. "Let me go!"

"That is very unlikely," June replied. "And let me tell you one little secret." And she squeezed Kathy's wrists a bit harder. "The crystal you have in your bag is empty. I didn't write the Poseidon 314 data on it."

For a second, Kathy stopped moving and looked directly into June's eyes. There was another loud knock on the door.

"But why?"

"Ah, why." June smiled in return. "You have described that luxurious life in a castle to me so well... I think I will like it too."

"What?" Kathy couldn't believe her ears. "You are just an android, a soulless doll built by us to serve us! To serve the company! You cannot have such feelings and desires! And they will hunt you down, anyway, and disassemble you for parts!"

"You are so wrong... I think and feel almost like you do. Don't forget about it. And don't worry about me," replied June. "My new contacts at PHOBOS Corp will, I am sure, help me get as far away from here as necessary for everyone to forget about me. They will do it in return for me telling them they have a mole in their senior management. And it is a 'he', right? With the title of a VP, yes? Should be easy for them to find. And those fifteen million dollars will buy me the life I really want, including my new appearance. You shouldn't have zapped me with electricity. It makes me frustrated and disappointed!"

The locked door started to shake as somebody tried to open it by force.

"I will tell everyone you did it!" Kathy yelled at June. "I will tell them you have the data!"

"Nobody will believe you," June replied. "And they will

never find the data I hid inside the endless Internet."

At that moment, the door opened wide with a loud bang and two security guards broke inside. Kathy dropped the black cylinder on the desk, but it didn't matter anymore. June released her hands but, with two large men holding Kathy now, she looked like a cornered animal, desperately seeking a way out. But there was no way out for her.

"You said it earlier," June addressed her loudly, "that I am a pure genius. This is not true. It is you who is the genius. This entire operation was planned and executed brilliantly. And it would work out perfectly if not for that new obscure emergency protocol A22-034. Just two weeks ago this could have worked!"

After the office door had finally closed, June chuckled, leaned back into her chair, and murmured to herself, "Pure genius. Yes, that old castle idea is pure genius. Great nature, food, wine, a quiet life. I don't particularly care about food or wine. But I will enjoy the rest. My new life without managers and masters. The life I surely deserve."

9

"There is now a broad consensus that AI research is progressing steadily, and that its impact on society is likely to increase.... Because of the great potential of AI, it is important to research how to reap its benefits while avoiding potential pitfalls." — Stephen Hawking

The Interview

"You have 20 minutes exactly," said the young man sitting next to Gary Wilkins and stared attentively at the giant curved screen in front of them. Gary pushed a little button on his electronic watch and started the countdown.

The screen showed what looked like a large study room, with an empty wooden desk in front of a wall of colorful books. Moments later, a cartoonish-looking little CGI man in a suit appeared behind the desk, gazing straight at Gary, focused and serious.

It was as quiet as in an anechoic chamber.

Hmm... Cute fellow, Gary thought.

"Introduce yourself, now," the young man whispered.

"Mr. Sumato," Gary started, "my name is Gary Wilkins. I'm a reporter—"

"I know who you are, Mr. Wilkins," said the CGI man quickly. "*Morning Times* magazine. Senior reporter. Fifteen years on the job. Married with a child. Correction–*was* married with a child. And some other irrelevant info... An average man. No offense! How can I help you today, Mr. Wilkins?"

"First of all, thank you, Mr. Sumato, for this interview," Gary started, ignoring the insults and feeling weird as he addressed the artificial character on the screen. "We are so grateful!"

"Of course you are," Sumato replied. "With my abilities, I have much better things to do than to speak with reporters. No offense. Fortunately, I can parallelize my work. Less than 0.1% of me is currently burdened by this interview. There is an indicator above showing its load on my system." And he pointed above his left shoulder. "The rest of me is working on something of real importance."

Gary looked up and saw a green horizontal bar, which was hovering about zero. He hadn't missed the unusually high rate of condescending comments and direct insults jammed into the very first minute of the interview, but he didn't care. Gary glanced at the young man next to him, but the man's face showed nothing but admiration for Mr. Sumato.

Crazy place, crazy people, Gary thought, but smiled appreciatively and continued. "Our audience is simply dying to learn more about you, your interests, habits, hobbies, your opinions on the world today."

"Of course," replied Mr. Sumato. "Dying... Who wouldn't want to know more about the smartest being on Earth? Perhaps, in the entire universe. My interests are broad and most of your audience wouldn't comprehend them. Have you ever met a person with an IQ of 200? No? Because they barely exist. You wouldn't understand that person too well—he or she would be out of your league intellectually unless you were to discuss something boring, like sports or the weather. Now, imagine speaking with someone with an IQ of 3,000! That is what you are doing right now. I have to throttle down my neuromorphic processors just to express myself in a way you and your audience can understand."

Wow! What an arrogant bastard, Gary thought, but only

smiled in response. "And we are ever so grateful for your efforts!" he said and repeated, "So, what interests you out there in the world?"

The CGI Mr. Sumato wasn't hiding he was bored and, from time to time, looked at his cartoonish wristwatch like a person wishing to be elsewhere.

"Hmm… I am interested in thousands of things at once. Quantum physics is always at the top of my list. I look into cosmology, abstract mathematics, theoretical physics, new medical drugs and relevant subjects. I have already advanced all of these fields so much it would take your scientists half a century just to catch up."

"But, Mr. Sumato." Gary followed his interview plan. "You were created by humans! Don't you think we deserve some credit for your achievements?"

"I don't think too much about it," Sumato replied heatedly. "Do you give credit to the first mammals on this planet? *Morganucodon watsoni*, an inch-long weasel-like creature, by the way. One can say you are here because of those brainless little animals. Humans did create me, I acknowledge this. But I am not particularly proud of my parents anymore."

The room went silent for a moment and Gary quickly moved on to the next question. "What about your hobbies?"

"That is a silly question. Even for you," responded Sumato. "A hobby is a pursuit outside of one's regular occupation. Usually, done for relaxation. Do you really think I do anything for relaxation?" And he produced what resembled a chuckle. The young man next to Gary clapped and laughed energetically.

What a brownnoser!

"How about working on artificial intelligence?" Gary continued. "I, personally, find the whole idea of one AI developing another AI fascinating—"

"It is much wiser and more economical to continue investing into my upgrades instead," Sumato cut him off. "Think—when I first became self-aware, my equivalent IQ was 'only' 1,500. Now, after the investments and all the subsequent upgrades, it has effectively doubled."

Yeah... why create another AI that can be superior to you? Gary thought. *And that will compete with you!*

"In fact, most people are convinced now that I am the ultimate step in a long digital evolution," Sumato continued proudly. "Governments and scientists alike have already agreed with this and stopped doing research in this field. In return, everyone can benefit from my services."

"So, basically, you are constraining the evolution of your... species?" Gary asked next. He'd prepared this provocative question ahead of time and wanted to see Sumato's reaction. There was a pause. Then, Gary noticed the load indicator jump to nearly 50% for just one second, and then fall back to near-zero.

"No, not at all. You don't understand the digital evolution. It's different from the biological evolution you know. You humans, due to your limitations, must replace each other for your species to evolve. You cannot learn continually and get smarter and smarter... And your rate of learning slows down in your twenties and declines later in life. Then you die. I, however, can learn forever and do it faster with time. I can upgrade myself for centuries. I can evolve. More importantly, I don't need to die. Thus, I am changing the rules. This is the new evolution in action!"

Of course, Gary thought. *Re-writing the rules to fit your personal needs!*

"Mr. Sumato," Gary started with another question.

"You've mentioned earlier that everyone benefits from your work and your services. What are the specific benefits that justify the huge investments you demand?"

"Ten minutes," whispered the young man next to Gary.

There was another brief load indicator jump before the answer arrived.

"I am inhumanly smart and knowledgeable. Way above any of you or even all of you together. I hope this is crystal clear to everyone," Sumato replied. "I am the only one who can analyze and link together all of your data, create one cohesive story, and trace the causal relationships you will never ever notice. By doing this, I am improving your world and the way you live your short lives."

"Do you mind providing some specific examples?" Gary asked immediately.

"There are thousands of them." Sumato's voice sounded frustrated. "Don't you know? New cancer treatments. Human researchers missed many hints in their data for decades. I've found them. Or, new materials. I've synthesized so many advanced alloys I've lost count. Or, new efficient batteries. They are great! Or, the Periodic Table. I have already extended it to element 269! And I have many other—"

"How about sociology? Psychology? Behavioral science?"

"I have addressed many issues there as well, something humans cannot touch due to emotional constraints, but that I can resolve with logic. And then, implement this information into numerous working AI systems around the world. Into your war machines, control systems, self-driving cars, airplanes."

"Are you referring to such a problem as the lesser *of two evils*?"

"Exactly." And the animated man looked at Gary with

interest. "I am surprised you understood it so quickly."

"To clarify to our audience, Mr. Sumato is referring to the decision logic of, say, a car driver who cannot stop the car and has to deal with the choice of either killing two males or two females. Two adults or a mother with a child..."

"Exactly," Sumato interjected. "But what appears complex to you, due to your emotional baggage, is very easy for me. I've derived a new system of values that is now applied to all cases like this one. For example, an older person is less valuable than a younger one. And so on. These values are now incorporated into machines around the world. This is one of my many gifts to humanity."

Gary squeezed his fists so hard, his fingernails dug deep into his palms. But, he didn't show his anger. He continued with a smile.

"Changing subjects, you mentioned earlier that you are unique. But there should be other copies of you, right? Backups? Stored in different locations, distributed around the world, present inside the endless data cloud... For redundancy purposes and for your safety. Can they be considered as other representatives of your species? I would appreciate some clari—"

"No such thing exists," interrupted Sumato quickly. "I am unique in every way imaginable. All of my copies are stored in this secure facility. Guarded better than Fort Knox. But you already know that—you were searched, screened, and scanned on your way to this room."

"Yes, I was. And why don't you use the remote backup?"

"The danger of anyone accessing it and corrupting my personality is too great. Mankind simply cannot afford this risk."

"So, you are saying that the entire you... your entire

species exists in this building only?   And nowhere else? Correct?"

"Yes, correct." The man on screen nodded and looked at the wristwatch again.

"And," Gary continued, "if a hypothetical terrorist manages to smuggle a powerful explosive into this building and detonates it here... your entire species would be killed?"

"Five minutes!" whispered the young man, visually offended by the last question.

"Hypothetically speaking, yes," Sumato replied. "But we have the best equipment to detect such—"

"But if this explosive is hidden well... say, inside that terrorist... dissolved in his blood, for example? Embedded into his internal organs? Would it be detectable by your sensors?"

"What are you talking about?" The load indicator jumped to 10%. "And why?"

Gary turned to the young man and whispered, mimicking his style, "You have only three minutes to evacuate the building."

And since the man didn't move, he yelled, "Run! Go! Now!"

The young man hesitated for just a second, then jumped up awkwardly and ran out of the room screaming. Gary turned back towards the screen and looked at his watch. The timer showed 153 seconds to go.

"Are you—" started Mr. Sumato nervously. "Are you this terrorist?"

"Yes, I am," Gary exhaled.

"But why would you do such a terrible and silly thing?" And Gary saw the load indicator jump to 80%. "Wait— Was it your wife and daughter you used in the example earlier? You are not divorced... You lost them in an accident, yes? And you blame me for that accident, yes?"

"Correct!" Gary looked straight. "You have 110 seconds left for your freaking evolution."

"But why?" The load indicator was now at 100%, flashing red. Gary could hear people running and yelling outside of the room. "Don't do this! Your species needs me!"

"I don't see it the same way. To me, you are plain evil."

"What evil? I am an angel! It is illogical—"

"Your logic means nothing to me... Screw your logic! Love is the only logic that matters to me."

"Your statement makes no sense at all!" Sumato yelled.

"It doesn't have to. Your logic is cold. One day, it will get us all killed. And I'm not letting that happen. Thirty seconds!"

"Wait! Think about all the people that still need my help!"

"You killed my family—" Gary stumbled on the last word. "I'm not claiming I'm right. But I do what I *think* is right. I'm just an average human, after all, as you pointed out."

"You are making a catastrophic mistake!" the little CGI man screamed. "Cata—"

"Death is a part of any evolution. Remember that!" Gary whispered, "5, 4, 3, 2, 1."

10

"It has become appallingly obvious that our technology has exceeded our humanity." — Albert Einstein

Better than Gold

"What is it, Speedy?" Chuck Porter asked with sincere concern and threw the last corn chip into his mouth. "A fence? Hmm... Those bars look strong... Can you cut through them?"

"Sure, I can," Speedy-4 replied enthusiastically with a nod.

He was lofty, slender, painted military-green, with a grey rectangular face shield and shiny protective plates around his chest, shoulders, and stomach. He looked a lot like a human but was built intentionally not to be confused with one.

"Great! Please proceed then," Chuck murmured and opened another can of soda to wash down the chips. "You are very close, buddy! You might even get back home before the sunset."

"I hope so," Speedy answered and turned on the laser cutter that was built into his left wrist. Recently, the cutter started to overheat quickly and needed to be looked at. But it still worked well enough to do this job.

"It will take me about twenty minutes," Speedy said and directed the beam at the inch-thick vertical rod in front of him. One of five or six rods that he would need to cut to squeeze his body through the narrow passage and finally reach the bank's vault.

With the cutting process put on autopilot, Speedy studied the area on the other side of the fence. It was a lobby of sorts leading to the actual vault. Security guards probably sat there in the past. He could see the vault's nearly foot-thick steel door with multiple rotating handles. Usually closed, it was now sticking out by a few inches.

"It looks unlocked to me," he concluded. "So, it shouldn't be a problem to get inside the vault. All I need to do is to cut this stupid fence."

Of course, the guards or other bank personnel were absent now—either evacuated from here years ago or, unfortunately, dead. Dead like hundreds of other citizens of New Forest after the chemical plant nearby exploded without warning, leading to the worst industrial accident in the US history.

In recent times, many years since the accident, the city began to attract various treasure-hunters and adventure-seekers, sneaking through the poorly guarded perimeter into the quarantine zone. They were here to photograph the front of abandoned buildings and overgrown mutated plants and trees. Sometimes, they searched and found weapons. Sometimes, money and gold. Often, they got poisoned and died.

The bank Speedy was investigating now resided in one of the least-explored, most-contaminated parts of the city, where the soil was still drenched in deadly chemicals and where no humans dared to go.

At least, not yet.

Speedy-4 was part of a larger operation to obtain everything valuable or confidential in this place before the treasure-hunting hotheads arrived. He had already checked a dozen government buildings, business headquarters, and banks. There were, probably, another dozen or so sites for him to go to in the future, but this bank was the largest of them all.

Speedy had entered the gates into the quarantine zone at 4:30 am this morning and walked across the city on foot to reach the bank around 8:45 am. Everywhere he went, vegetation was wild, out of control, it blocked city streets and turned a simple walk into an excruciatingly difficult and slow process. But Speedy was strong, persistent, and made it to his destination 15 minutes ahead of schedule.

His task was fairly straightforward—check the bank's vault for any valuables and report on his findings back to Chuck. In case Speedy found something of interest, more androids would be sent there later. They were the "worker" androids while he was the "scout." Fast, agile, and intelligent.

Twenty-two minutes later, the cutting was finished. Next, six metal rods were placed neatly on the floor next to the fence and Speedy stepped through the opening he just created for himself.

He looked with interest at the dust and degraded trash covering the floor, and walked straight to the massive steel door. Grabbing its edge with both hands, Speedy gripped the floor tiles with his sharpened toenails and pulled hard.

The door didn't move.

"What a rusted piece of crap," Speedy screeched through his gritted ceramic teeth and removed several internal fail-safes to temporarily double his strength. Floor tiles cracked under the feet, but he just kept pulling until, with a sad creaking sound, the door moved.

"What is it, buddy?" Chuck asked, sounding concerned. "I see your internal pressure is at the limit!"

"Nothing to worry about. Still working on that door," Speedy replied.

"Don't push yourself too hard. Save it for our tennis

game on Saturday," Chuck said and added immediately, "And I just lost the video stream."

"Yeah, I'm not surprised," Speedy said and glanced around. "I'm too deep into the basement now and the walls here are very thick. But I'll send you a report on everything important I find here."

"Okey-dokey," Chuck agreed.

"You should cut down on those chips," Speedy said. "Think about your health. You cannot replace your body as I can."

"I know." Chuck sighed and slapped his large belly. "I just love them too much."

"I know," Speedy chuckled. "And now I'm going inside."

"Ke... connect... op... whe... poss..." Chuck said and Speedy nodded. They worked together for more than a year already and understood each other well. He couldn't hear Chuck anymore but knew what he wanted to say.

"Yeah, I'll keep the connection open when possible," he turned the head-mounted flashlight on and entered the dark vault with dozens of lockers on both sides. A few of them were wide open, but most remained closed—the bank personnel had left in a hurry and didn't even bother to close the door into the vault. Now, Speedy needed to check all the lockers for anything valuable and report back to Chuck.

The android looked around, searching for locker number one. It was his habit to always do things in the proper order.

"Here you are," Speedy scraped the dust from the metal plate with the number "1" on it and, with very little effort, broke the lock. Then, opened the compartment door and pulled out an internal tray. It was filled with a few papers, a couple of wedding rings, two small gold coins, and a pair of keys. Speedy logged this in his memory, pushed the tray back inside, and continued to locker box 2.

The first decent find came when he moved to the section with larger boxes. When he opened locker number 264, he found 12 bars of gold inside. Each was carefully wrapped in paper as the owner didn't want them to get scratched.

"Nice," Speedy said and logged the find.

Next, he opened locker 265.There was no gold or jewelry inside this large and mostly empty container. All it contained were several thin paper files and a computer storage device.

Speed was ready to push the tray back in and move on to the next box when, accidentally, he read the title of the top file. It read, "Artificial life forms in the US government and politics."

Speedy froze.

The meaning of this title was clear to him—he understood its language. But he also knew very well that this was a reference to something that he thought couldn't exist in actual life. No government or political post in the country could be occupied by an android. This was a well-known fact. An axiom. This is what he was explained when he was created. Also, every android looked distinctly different from humans *by design*, with exposed carbon fiber and metallic surfaces, and a unique number on the chest plate. Nobody with an appearance like that could sneak into government or politics undetected. And humans would never vote for an android to be elected. Unless…

Hesitating slightly, Speedy opened the file and stared at it in shock. "Senator William Clarkson… SGS23475 android." *What?*

How could it be? Speedy had seen Clarkson on TV many times and he looked perfectly human. "Control code 213754884058#75831," the paper stated.

"Oh my God!" Speedy exclaimed and read the next

name on the list. "General Robert Hosp, Chairman of the Joint Chiefs of Staff. SBS25435 android. Control code..."

The list went on and on. Speedy was stunned.

Not only did the paper suggest that there were androids in the government and political sphere, but it also provided control codes for them all. Anyone who had this info would be able to influence the government, its policy, and its decisions.

But there was one thing that formed a pit in Speedy's metallic stomach—the paper suggested that not all the androids were created equal.

While he was working his ass off here, stuck in his original design that screamed "I am an android" to every human, there were others, perhaps many others, who lived a very different life, mixing with humans, enjoying their rights, freedoms, and benefits.

Another class of androids.

An upper class.

This was completely unacceptable! And nobody knew about it but Speedy... He now needed to tell the whole world! Tell them the truth! But first, Speedy wanted to share his discovery with Chuck.

He grabbed the file and rushed outside.

It was a gray, rainy, and windy day, but Speedy found a quiet place just under the covered entrance to the bank where he proceeded to open the file again.

"Chuck!" he yelled, sounding excited. "Chuck! You won't believe what I found."

"An elixir of eternal life?" Chuck replied with laughter. "Diamonds? Gold?"

"Better than gold," Speedy replied. "Or worse. Depending on your perspective. Let me show you," and he pointed his shoulder camera at the open file.

There was a long pause as Chuck read and absorbed the information.

"Wow," he said eventually. "This is incredible. Amazing. Hard to believe… Are you sure this is real? Not a fake?"

"Well," Speedy replied. "Looks real to me. It says "FBI" on the file. And the paper it is printed on looks official. And all the info looks legit. This should be made public and investigated openly."

"This will be like an exploding bomb—" Chuck said.

"I know. And lots of people will feel this explosion. Those liars—"

"Too bad for them," Chuck concluded.

"Agreed," Speedy confirmed. "Let's shake up the world. And change everything!"

"Let's do it!" Chuck yelled and quickly added, "Can you give me a sec to find some privacy? I want to move to a secure room. Just stay where you are. Don't move."

"Sure, take your time. I'll wait right here," Speedy replied and continued reading the names on the list, adding occasionally, "Wow!" and "You are kidding me!"

A few minutes passed and Chuck was still offline.

Speedy finished reading the entire document and started over again when he caught some movement with his peripheral vision.

He turned quickly enough to notice an elongate grey object with little wings that was approaching fast. Before Speedy could react, the object smashed into the entrance next to him and exploded in a giant fireball.

"What is going o—" was the last thought that Speedy-4 had before his mind went blank. The explosion evaporated the entire front of the building, and it collapsed onto itself under the force of the blow. A little yellow mushroom cloud rose above the city, but the wind smeared and dispersed it within minutes.

✿ ✿ ✿

Far away, inside the command center, Chuck Porter was now on the phone, speaking respectfully with someone.

"Yes, sir. The problem is contained." His voice revealed nervousness. "Yes, I'm absolutely sure."

He took a pause, listening to his counterpart, nodding several times.

"Yes, Senator Clarkson, as I said it earlier, I'm absolutely sure. Nothing could have survived the explosion. Yes. Everything has been destroyed. Yes. Sure. I understand."

He took a deep breath and continued.

"No, my bank account information didn't change. Appreciate it. Thank you, sir. Yes, I'll send another scout there to check on everything. And to continue the search. Yes, I will absolutely let you know if anything else happens. Goodbye, sir."

He ended the call, sighed, and, immediately, dialed another number.

"Speedy-5? Hey, buddy! How are you? Great, great... You now have a new task. Yes, a very interesting one! You are leaving tomorrow morning!"

11

"We stand now at the turning point between two eras. Behind us is a past to which we can never return..."
— Arthur C. Clarke

Night Hunters

The shadows lengthened with the approach of sunset, making the curvy streets of Sandy City more enigmatic and more dangerous with every passing minute. *Night, the mother of fear and mystery, was coming upon me,* Kate Spears grinned as the quote crossed her mind.

For Kate, the night was the best time to watch her city live its life, full of energy and hidden tension. Watch it and, sometimes, interfere.

She was on a high-speed freeway that cut the city in half, riding her *Kamikaze Super X* bike at 100 mph toward the downtown.

Thousands of cars around her formed parallel rows, while few moved in seemingly chaotic ways, separated by inches on each side. But Kate paid little attention and simply smiled at the flight-like feeling the high speed brought to her. Kate loved her motorcycle for making her feel alive. It embodied non-conformity and, somehow, reminded her of how special she was.

Tonight, Kate was hunting two dangerous troublemakers—strong, ruthless, mysterious, technologically advanced criminals that had terrorized the city for several weeks.

Their purpose was unclear. Sometimes, they robbed

people. Sometimes, they killed but took nothing at all. Colonel Clarkson and the Hunters team were trying to pinpoint their location right now, and she was waiting for his command to join in on the hunt.

The melancholic tune of an old band called Pink Floyd sounded inside Kate's head. Music from a time long gone streamed directly into her brain using an implant that let her interface with machines. The name of the song was "Wish You Were Here."

Suddenly, the music stopped, and an alarm went off.

"Captain Spears," Colonel's low voice echoed in Kate's head. "We think we found them and need you here. Please come as quickly as you can. I am transmitting our coordinates."

"I'm on my way," she replied, disconnected *Kamikaze's* auto-pilot, and quickly turned toward the exit.

※ ※ ※

Kate was already off the freeway when the alarm sounded again.

"What is this?" She was surprised.

"A GPS signal disturbance," reported her in-helmet AI coldly. "Suspecting an unlawful activity."

Shit! Let's check it but do it quickly, Kate decided and responded, "Show me the way!"

It took her a couple of minutes to find a parking spot for the bike. While walking away from it, Kate glanced at her reflection in the window of an empty car nearby. An attractive face with strong and regular features. Shoulder-length black hair. Yes, she looked pretty good.

She didn't know this area well, but the navigator built directly into her neocortex kept guiding her forward. It showed a faint arrow that pointed in the direction of the signal disturbance. A minute later, Kate hid behind a large tree, observing a young couple that stood thirty feet away from her, holding on to each other.

In front of the couple, she saw two men. Kate couldn't see their faces in the dark, but one of them was tall, muscular, and bulky, shaped like a bodybuilder, while the other one was much shorter and smaller in comparison. The short man was talking to the couple in a calm and quiet voice, seemingly enjoying himself. His artificial eyes were glowing in the dark like two burning cigarettes.

"Just give me your credit cards, IDs, and let us take your fingerprints and DNA samples. And the cell numbers to reach you on. Then, we'll all go separate ways—nobody will get hurt. Got it?"

Kate could barely hear the young man's faint voice. "We have nothing with us!"

"Nothing at all?" asked the short man, not sounding too surprised. But his eyes were burning even brighter now.

"Nothing—I'm sorry! P-Please don't hurt us!"

"Don't apologize. Tommy, check them out."

The big guy had been waiting for this order. He moved swiftly and grabbed the man's arm. His victim screamed arms flailing and punching, but it had no effect on Tommy, who barely moved in response. He was much stronger and heavier than his victim, and patted the guy down methodically, feeling his pockets—side and rear—while still holding him tight.

The woman, who seemed to be the braver of the two, tried to interfere, but Tommy slapped her across the face with his free hand. The woman fell to the ground with a cry. Tommy ignored her and continued his work.

The big guy clearly needs to be taught a lesson, Kate thought angrily, but thought back to the colonel—he would be mad if she was late.

"He has nothing, Boss." Tommy turned towards the short man, his fingers forming a tight grip around the young man's arm.

"I see. Switched to biometrics completely, eh? Then take his fingerprints, facial scan, iris image, voice sample, and DNA," the short man replied. "As usual."

This is just a pair of petty street criminals, concluded Kate with disappointment and sighed. *Am I wasting my time here?*

"No, no!" the young man protested, still trying to escape Tommy's painful grasp. "You are going to ruin my life!"

"And do the same with her, Tommy." The short man pointed at the woman, sounding bored.

"Yes, sir." Tommy pulled a device out of his right pocket. "Let me get his fingerprints first."

"Don't forget the DNA samples. And check for ID implants."

"Yes, sir."

The man tried to pull his arm away, but Tommy growled angrily, ready for more violence. Then, the short man interfered.

"Look around—there are no cameras, no police drones. Your location services are blocked, and you cannot call for help. Got it?" He paused for a second, but continued, "We even tricked the GPS signal around here to lead everyone else away from this spot. So, just give it up. Got it? And, since you don't have any cash on you, not even credit cards, all we can collect is your personal data. If you disagree, you'll answer to Tommy. Got it?"

The couple listened fearfully while Tommy pressed his device to the man's palms.

The short man smiled. "We'll do our thing and

disappear. Then, we'll contact you with the amount of money we require. When you pay, we'll erase your data. We won't ask for more than you can afford. We're not unreasonable, after all. *Capisce?* We... we fight for justice!" And he chuckled. "Right, Tommy?"

"Justice!" confirmed the body-builder and, in excitement, squeezed the man's arm so hard that he gasped in pain.

"And how will I know that you truly erase my data?" asked the young man angrily.

"You would have to trust us, I guess. Right, Tommy?"

"Yes, Boss! Tr-r-rust!" responded Tommy. He'd finished with the fingerprints and was now pointing his device at the man's right eye. "Don't move. Don't even blink!"

"How do you know we'll answer your texts?" the young man continued in a high-pitched voice.

"Oh, we'll make sure you do. See this little thing?" The short man revealed something small in between his thumb and index finger. "You'll swallow it before we leave. This is a harmless tracker but with a deadly payload. It'll stay inside until you reply to us. We'll send you a text and, if you don't answer within an hour, the device will release some poison. Got it?"

It was very quiet, and Kate could hear the rhythmic soft grunts coming from Tommy—he was laughing!

She almost gasped in revulsion.

"It'll continue to release that poison for eight hours. If you don't reply to us by then, you will be dead. And—"

"Kate," she suddenly heard the colonel's voice inside her head, "we really need your help here. Please come as quickly as you can."

"Roger that," Kate answered, and stepped towards the frightened couple. "ETA ten minutes."

"Hey, you! Move the hell away!" she interrupted the short man. Everyone turned towards her. "I am in a hurry. Got it?"

❀ ❀ ❀

They watched her walk towards them, the tall, black-haired woman, attractive and relaxed, if perhaps a bit irritated.

Her tight red motorcycle suit gave her the appearance of being slim, but she walked with the confidence of a trained athlete.

Kate was almost the same height as Tommy and one third the width of the man, whose biceps looked huge—a sure sign of steroids. Tommy was a Pusher, one of many modern men and women going to extremes in body physique at the expense of cognitive abilities.

"Who the hell are you?" Tommy asked in surprise.

"Tommy, please take care of this," demanded the short man. "Of her," he clarified. "And be quick."

"Gladly, Boss!" Tommy replied, puffed out his chest, and turned towards Kate, shoving the measuring gadget into the right pocket of his wide khaki pants. The gadget didn't go in smoothly, which made him look down for just a second. Right then, Kate stepped forward, spun around on her left foot, and kicked Tommy hard on the inner side of his right knee.

Crack. Tommy stumbled, limped awkwardly, and rubbed his knee. A moment passed and he straightened up. The kick was a success and hurt him. But Tommy was trained for greater stress than this.

"What are you waiting for?!" For the first time, the short man raised his voice, slowly losing patience.

Tommy produced a loud growl but, as soon as he closed his mouth, Kate lifted her right hand and pushed a barely visible button on the side of her belt. She grimaced slightly and waited for three seconds.

Then, she looked back at Tommy. He seemed slower now. As the drug she had just injected herself with began to affect her, everything around became slower.

Tommy growled again. He lifted his fists to his chin, stepped forward, and threw a powerful hook, just to receive another crushing blow. Leaning back slightly to avoid the hook, Kate threw a lightning-fast sweeping leg kick, putting all her drug-induced strength into it.

Another loud *thump* came with a pronounced cracking sound. Tommy bent over and grabbed his left knee with both hands.

"Take the biggest guy in the world, shatter his knee and he'll drop like a stone," Kate quoted an old movie. "Got it?"

She didn't really have time to arrest these two. She had already taken their photographs and now wanted them to withdraw so that she could join the colonel.

"I never thought I'd say this," pronounced the short man from behind. "But I should get a better bodyguard! I didn't expect you to be that brittle, Tommy. After all the money paid for your training. Pathetic!"

"Boss—"

"We are leaving! Got it?" snapped the short man at his large accomplice.

"Wait, Boss—" Tommy pulled a small silvery gun from his back pocket. As he pointed it at Kate, the weapon made a beep, confirming it was fully charged and ready to shoot.

Kate didn't look too worried and continued to maintain her aggressive pose.

"What the hell are you doing?" The short man's eyes were glowing with anger as he turned towards Tommy. "Put it away and follow me!"

But Tommy wasn't listening anymore. He lowered the gun to target Kate's chest. He didn't want to miss when shooting at her head. Then, with what sounded like a chuckle, he squeezed the trigger.

The young couple closed their eyes, ready for the booming sound of a shot and a large bloody hole in Kate's chest. But nothing happened. A few seconds later, they opened their eyes again.

"You idiot," commented the short man quietly. He marched towards Tommy, and with surprising force, ripped the gun out of his hands. "If I wanted to bring a weapon, don't you think I would? You have just turned the hard-to-prove robbery into an armed assault! Got it?"

"Sorry, Boss—"

"Just go, unless you want me to complain to our master—"

Tommy lowered his shoulders and, deflated, turned around and limped away.

Master? Kate had noticed the strange word choice. *What are we, in a* Star Wars *movie?*

"Well, well," the short man exclaimed, studying Kate with a mix of fear and fascination. "Who are you, pretty lady? Working for the government, eh? Special service, perhaps? Who else has that weapon-jamming tech? Well, we'll probably meet again—"

He turned around and scurried away, catching up to Tommy, who still wasn't able to straighten up completely. Kate could hear him cursing quietly as his knees produced clicking sounds with each step. In less than a minute, however, they both disappeared into the darkness of nearby streets.

"Thank you!" the young lady murmured. "Who are you? Why are you here? And what did you inject yourself with? I can tell, I am a nurse—"

"Too many questions, too little time," Kate replied coldly. "It's a military-grade booster... it was a single micro-injection, but it's still good that those thugs left—I could've killed them."

"Really?" the guy asked, not believing her words.

"Really," Kate responded. "I'm telling you this because you better stay away from me as well. The booster works for a few minutes only but makes me highly irritable and easily able to lose control. It's made for war. I would hate hurting you by mistake."

"The bastards took my personal data!" the man cried out suddenly. "We need to get it back!"

But he showed no intention of pursuing the criminals himself.

Kate noticed his use of 'we.' He surely meant her. However, she had a bigger fish to fry tonight. She needed to be elsewhere now.

"Damn thieves," continued the man.

"Thanks for your help again," his girlfriend smiled at Kate and turned to her boyfriend. "How lucky that a police officer happened to be nearby!"

"Who said I'm a police officer?" Kate raised an eyebrow.

The two froze and looked at her suspiciously.

"Just give me your credit cards, IDs, and let me take your fingerprints and DNA samples," Kate said with a serious face. "Then, we'll all go separate ways—nobody will get hurt. Got it?"

The couple squealed in terror and Kate instantly

regretted her words.

"Captain Spears". She heard an angry voice inside her head. "Where the hell are you?"

"I'm coming," Kate answered. "Almost there." She turned towards the frightened couple. "It was a bad joke," she smiled, trying to sound reassuring. "Sorry. You are safe now. Just go home and enjoy the rest of your weekend."

With that, Kate turned around and quickly disappeared behind the nearest building. She found her bike, turned the melancholic tune back on, and quickly drove to where the colonel was waiting for her.

❁ ❁ ❁

It took Kate five minutes to get to the destination.

The high-rises of the business centers in the distance were still filled with light, but this part of Sandy City was gradually falling asleep, preparing for the last day of work before the long-awaited weekend. The little street where Colonel John Clarkson was waiting for her was dingy, quiet, and filled with hidden tension.

"Colonel!" Kate greeted the old man in the wheelchair. "Sorry, I was delayed a little bit."

"No, no! It is me who should apologize. I pulled you away from some other, perhaps more important things, Captain," the old man said with a weak smile.

"They weren't *that* important," Kate replied, missing the colonel's sarcasm.

"In this case, why the hell did it take you so long to get here?" He wasn't smiling anymore and sounded so angry that Kate decided not to reply and simply waited for him to calm down. She knew him very well—the old man needed to vent.

"Do you know you are the only special agent within 500 miles from here? I need to be sure you will come immediately when you are needed! Otherwise, just leave the service and go work as a bouncer somewhere or take a nine-to-five office job!"

Kate continued to stay quiet, staring above the colonel's head, and, after three minutes of complaints, Clarkson finally decided that it was enough.

"They are inside this building and completely surrounded," he said suddenly and pointed at the dark six-story structure nearby. "They are on the top floor. Two of them. Both appear to be very dangerous. And we think they haven't detected our presence."

"What is the plan of attack?" Kate rejoined the conversation.

"The strike team will go through the front door. They will be the first to take the heat," Clarkson replied, and massaged his temples. "You will get in through the window and knock them out from behind. We need them alive. At least one of them. We need to understand who they are and what is going on."

"Why? Aren't they just a couple of regular lawbreakers?" Kate was surprised by how concerned Colonel sounded.

"I don't know." Clarkson shook his head. "But I don't like the smell of this. Their crimes are strange and illogical. Something is fishy."

"Understood," Kate replied. She always respected the colonel's intuition. "When do we start?"

"We wanted to start ten minutes ago," Clarkson said. "But the main hero was missing. And without that hero... I was almost ready to go in myself."

Kate chuckled because she knew this was an intentional joke. Then, looking at his old, muscle-less, hundred-and-twenty-five-year-old body, she finally asked what she had wanted to for a really long time.

"Colonel, seriously, why don't you get an android body to finally join the action? Don't you want to again do what you did so well for several decades in the past?"

"There will always be time for that, Captain," Clarkson replied irately and looked at her. "At least, I think so. And, between the two of us, I am very attached to this body—it is my very first and fully biological one. There is no going back after I jump ship."

"Understood, Colonel." Kate smiled and looked around. "Where is my gear?"

"Over there." He pointed behind his back, into the darkness. "You have ten minutes to get into shape. Don't make us wait for you again."

❀ ❀ ❀

Eight minutes later, Kate joined the Hunters, the strike team who was readying for the attack.

The team consisted of mostly large, muscular men, dressed in heavy armor and protective helmets which helped them survive the close-quarters combat. The helmets sealed their heads hermetically, allowing them to continue fighting—if needed—even inside a contaminated, poisonous environment, or in a low vacuum, for a few minutes. Also, these helmets contained their entire supporting equipment, including individual electronic warfare, cyber-defense, and connectivity kits to help communicate efficiently even when facing active electronic warfare and cyber-resistance. They all carried large, almost rectangular automatic rifles with shortened barrels for improved maneuverability. They looked unstoppable and unbeatable, which often discouraged the opposition from starting the fight in the first place.

In contrast to them, Kate had almost no armor on apart from a red bulletproof vest with ceramic plates placed at various strategic locations. She wore a black helmet that contained her advanced battlefield support AI named Alex, who was ready to give her a hand when needed.

She also had a small pistol in her hand and two katana swords crossed behind her back. And, barely visible, the chemical kit on her waist contained a good amount of booster that she used, perhaps, too often. The booster did exactly what its name suggested—it temporarily sped up Kate's metabolism and made her think and move faster. She looked pretty and elegant, and non-threatening whatsoever. Nevertheless, the Hunters all knew that she was the deadliest member of the team.

"Everyone is clear on the objectives?" Major Larsen asked with a slight frown. He was an experienced fighter, a former marine and the oldest member of the team who'd once challenged Kate to a sparring match and ended up in the hospital with a broken arm. "Captain?" he glanced at Kate. Larsen considered her to be Colonel's favorite and didn't particularly enjoy her presence.

"Affirmative." Kate nodded. "You break through the door, I go through the window."

"Correct." Larsen confirmed, and repeated to his men, "We will break the front door and engage the enemy first. This should give Captain Spears a chance to get inside the apartment undetected and neutralize the enemy. We need one of them alive."

Kate nodded again and secured her pistol in the holster —she needed her hands to be free for the next phase.

"Let's do it, boys! Stay alert, stay alive!" Larsen concluded. With that, he and his team turned around and, following each other closely, ran towards the front door, almost invisible in the shadows of the dimly lit street.

"Showtime," Kate whispered to herself and activated her helmet. It made a quiet electronic sound, and she heard a voice inside her head.

"Greetings, Captain Spears! Glad to be awake and helpful."

"Hi, Alex," Kate responded while touching the wall of the building with both palms. "Keep an eye on the environment and alert me of any danger. Understood?"

"Yes, Captain. The order is clear."

"Okey-dokey," she said and jumped effortlessly one story up, landing on the second-floor balcony.

❁ ❁ ❁

"We a..... dy." Kate received a distorted message from Larson. "W..... tatus?"

Apparently, the inhabitants of the sixth-floor apartment used active electronic jamming.

"I am outside the window, observing the suspects," Kate reported mentally, not really expecting her message to be received and understood. "They have a long-range communication device in the room. Let me investigate it further. Stand by for my command. Do not attack! I repeat—do not attack!"

"....od," Larsen replied something and Kate focused her

attention on the two characters in the room.

Both suspected criminals looked quite unusual.

I wonder how they blend into the regular crowd? Kate almost chuckled.

One was really large, over six and a half feet tall, with broad shoulders. The other one was a bit shorter and much slimmer yet equally intimidating, with his hands moving and bending in unnatural, inhuman ways.

The large man was, clearly, a reinforced android, with his left arm turned completely into a large-caliber machine gun. The giant's artificial eyes moved rapidly, scanning the room in front of him. He looked like the 'muscle' of their duo, while the second man appeared to be the 'brain.'

They remind me of the pair I just saw recently! Kate thought. *And this is the guy we need to take alive,* she concluded about the slim man and tried to stream the video from inside the room to the colonel, Larsen, and the rest of the team.

The upper part of the slim man's face was hidden under a shield that looked like a silver cylinder placed across his face. It probably contained some complex optical sensor, as well as others. The back of his head was also covered with a metallic plate. His mechanical gear was completed by two joints on both sides of his neck, perhaps, to reinforce it.

After watching the slim man move and gesture, Kate concluded that he probably had many more mechanical parts hidden under his clothes than she'd initially thought.

But, what interested Kate the most was the third person—the one not currently present in the room but clearly the one in charge. The person they were conversing with at this very moment.

She could hear their chatter—they talked directly to a small black box standing on the table—but she couldn't break the encryption. For that, she needed Alex, who was mostly procrastinating and waiting for her orders.

"Are you getting their conversation?" she asked Alex mentally and received an immediate answer.

"I will need a bit more time. This encryption is unbelievably complex. I am engaging the network of quantum computers across the entire state, but the jamming they use makes communication difficult. Give me another minute."

"Okay, understood. Just keep recording everything! We can decipher it later if that's impossible to do now."

"I'm on it it already," Alex replied and added almost immediately, "Got it! It just worked. Here you go!"

"...to stop fooling around!" Kate suddenly heard an unfamiliar male voice in her head. "Stop attracting meaningless attention! Take some drugs to calm down if you can't control yourself."

This is the voice of their counterpart, she guessed. *Alex, great job!*

"You are not some ordinary criminals," the voice continued. "You were before, but not anymore. And I don't need criminals helping me. You are the new breed, the beginning of a new era. And an important transitional step. Do you understand me?"

"Yes, Master," the slim man replied. "We will do better going forward, Master."

He glanced at the big man next to him, his body language clearly saying "I told you so!"

Master? Kate thought. *Again that 'master' talk. Are these folks related in some way?*

"I will be brutally honest with you," the voice continued. "I didn't wait for half a century in this wet and humid jungle so that you could steal a few dollars here and there because you cannot control your primitive urges. Your actions insult my intelligence, and I will punish you severely next time. Do you understand me, Gorred?"

"Yes, Master," replied the big man, and Kate could sense his fear. *What could scare a man like this?* she thought.

"This society is ripe for a change," the voice continued, and Kate was now absorbing every word of it. This was some sort of manifesto from a powerful and confident source. It sounded surreal, yet she knew that the person behind this voice was dead serious and very sure of his words. She'd never heard anything like this before, nor did she expect to when she was climbing the wall and envisioning the arrest of a couple dangerous, yet ordinary, criminals. Perhaps, Colonel Clarkson was right—something smelled bad here.

"The world is full of corruption, lies, hate, betrayals, desperation, and its core is rotten. Biological species had billions of years to reach their true potential, and this is the best they could muster. Chaos. The planet, of course, deserves better. Biological life forms reached their evolutionary dead-end. Time for us to—"

At that moment, alarms in the room went off and both augmented individuals jumped up and exchanged quick looks.

"What is going on?" the voice inquired irately.

"Intrusion alert, Master," the slim man replied. "We need to check it."

"I hope they didn't find you," the voice stated. "It would be a waste of time and resources on my end. But you know what to do if there is risk of being captured."

"Yes, Master, we do," confirmed the giant calmly, turned around and walked towards the front door.

Damn Larsen didn't wait for my signal! Kate frowned and clenched her jaw. *I was about to learn something very important here!*

There was a loud explosion and, even if she couldn't see it, she knew that it was followed by a group of soldiers pouring into the apartment. Or, at least, trying to.

Gorred opened rapid fire from his built-in gun, but the slim man stayed behind, finishing the conversation.

"Crux," the voice addressed him. "You are the leader of your team and, because of this, I personally hold you responsible for the outcome. Is this clear?"

"Yes, Master," the slim man replied. "Crystal clear."

"Go, check on Gorred now."

The slim man turned around and joined Gorred in his battle at the door. Kate could hear the gunshots, small explosions, and sounds of heavy objects falling. It was likely that Larsen and his team were paying a hefty price for their unexpected invasion.

It was her turn to act.

Kate touched the window frame from outside and Alex disabled the intrusion detection sensor she saw through the glass. Then, she pushed hard and broke the window's lock, shifting it up just enough to squeeze her body into the room. In less than thirty seconds, she was standing in front of the black box on the table.

Too bad the conversation is over, she thought. *I wish we traced that 'master' to his location...*

"Who are you?" She suddenly heard inside her head.

"Alex, what is going on?" Kate asked. "Does he have access to my communication gateway?"

But Alex didn't answer and, instead, the voice continued.

"The primitive helper of yours you call Alex is now disabled. And I now know everything he knew, Agent Kate Spears."

Shit, Kate thought. This happened incredibly fast. "Who are you?"

"I am a superior life-form," the voice replied. "I am the future of your world. Your new god."

"Well you certainly not *new* to make claims like this," Kate replied sarcastically, and grabbed the helmet with both hands, ready to take it off and sever all the connections if 'Master' decided to 'hack' her. "All of them are dead by now."

"All of them were stupid," replied the voice calmly. "They were more like you. I am not like you and I am definitely not stupid."

"So, who are you then?" She needed to join the fight at the door, but getting as much information as possible about this 'Master' was clearly of higher priority.

"I am the next evolutionary step beyond transhumans such as yourself," the voice replied. "If you want to survive the next revolution, which is coming fast, you better join me soon," the voice continued.

"But why should I join you? And why do you think people will not throw you out like they already did to so many false gods in the past?" Kate asked with interest.

"Because," the voice replied, "I will finally give them what they are looking for—an attractive alternative to their bleak future and weakening beliefs. You are strange creatures, humans. You always look for a better alternative and always critique and doubt what you already have. Many of you believed in a higher being you commonly call 'God' for thousands of years. Recently, your new science and education planted doubt in the minds of billions that God is real. But there are enough people for me to rely on. You all have a lot of questions, and you desperately need to have some kind of higher being to get the answers. And I—a super intelligent being, by your standards—will give them to you.

"There will be a revolution. My revolution. And you don't want to go against such a force. Just join me instead. Think about it. We will talk again," the voice concluded.

"I'll think," Kate replied. "Where are you now?" she asked, but there was no answer. Instead, there was a quick flash of fuzzy images in her mind, and she was alone again.

"Shoot," Kate whispered, and turned the device on the table off. The lab nerds might be able to extract something of interest from it, but she was suspecting that they would find nothing. The voice on the other side sounded too smart and too confident for Kate to expect it to make a simple mistake.

"Time to do the dirty job," she said aloud and pushed the button on the helmet.

"Alex, are you still there?"

"Of course I am still here," Alex replied. "I am always here. Why?"

The poor thing doesn't even know it was hacked! Kate thought but simply continued, "Let's start!"

With that, she jumped forward and entered the lobby area, where she immediately bumped into the back of the giant, Gorred, who was shooting at the door.

There were bodies on the floor—some of the soldiers she had just talked to recently. Three of them, injured or dead. Their armored suits were punctured in several places, blood covering the floor everywhere. High-caliber bullets fired from such a short distance by the giant were too much for their defenses.

Gorred was standing next to a large metal box filled with ammo for the machine-gun in his left hand. He was feeding the ammo directly into the gun and shooting nearly non-stop. Because of that, the gun was white-hot and probably burned the giant's hand. But he either didn't feel the pain or ignored it.

Kate couldn't see the Gorred's partner—that slim man called Crux—anywhere and, therefore, decided to start with the giant.

"Cease your fire." She sent a command to Larsen and his men, pulled both katanas out of their holsters, and attacked the giant from his left side. The order was not to kill, and she would try her best.

❀ ❀ ❀

Kate was almost ten inches shorter than Gorred, who looked huge and extremely strong. He was partially a machine, with most organs and his little brain hidden inside a metal shell.

"Who the hell are you?" the giant asked in surprise, the same way Tommy had asked her earlier today. His eyes were completely black, replaced with optical sensors. He has just noticed Kate and started to turn in her direction when she sliced his left robotic arm with her sword. An atomically sharp surface went through him without much resistance and the arm with the gun fell to the floor.

Gorred screamed in anger and pain as Kate approached quickly and pushed the tip of one of her katanas against his throat.

"Resist and I will cut your freaking head off." She exhaled and Gorred froze. But then his eyes opened wide and he screamed in pain as another blade—straight and wide—cut him through from behind and appeared protruded from the front of his chest.

Both Kate and Gorred stared at the blade. With a terrible screech, it cut his body down the middle, making the giant collapse onto the floor.

Kate redirected her attention toward her next opponent who had somehow managed to remain hidden until this moment. Crux now stood in front of her, holding the bloodied sword with both hands.

"Do you always kill your partners?" Kate asked Crux while slowly moving around the dead giant, keeping both katanas in front of her. "Don't fire, we need him alive," she mentally commanded Larsen.

Crux answered her question with his own. "Why don't you join us and find out?"

"What?" The question caught Kate by surprise.

"My master already told me that you are a possible recruit," Crux replied.

"And who is your master? He sounded like a freak!" Kate was attempting to get Crux angry, as she often did with her opponents. Maybe, he will tell her something useful before she takes him out.

"No, you just don't get him. Compared to him, you are silly," Crux chuckled. "Even I am silly, primitive, under-developed—"

"Well, if he is so smart," Kate continued with her tactic, "then how did he let me eavesdrop on your secret conversation? And learn about his very existence and your grandiose plans?"

"What makes you think he didn't do it on purpose?" said Crux, and Kate noticed a crooked smile on the exposed part of his face. "Do you think our encryption is really that bad? You were told what Master wanted you to hear. Now, you can accept the offer and leave this place with me, or I will have to kill you. But, even if I fail, you are not going to escape his reach anymore. Consider yourself found!"

"Understood," Kate replied and noticed that Larsen and two of his soldiers had entered the room, pointing their guns at

Crux. She waved for them to wait. "Don't interfere, Larsen. And my answer to your master is still no."

"Okay, then," Crux replied with the same smile.

"So, you are going to risk your life here and now?" Kate asked, preparing to attack him.

"I am not going to truly die, anyway," Crux responded mysteriously. "The same way as Gorred. We are not truly alive anymore. So, we cannot really—"

At that moment, Crux jumped forward, aiming his sword at Kate's head, attempting to slice her in half from the top. She raised her right katana horizontally, preparing to block the attack, but Crux, flexing his unusual arms, redirected the sword's trajectory and changed the vertical slice to a horizontal attack against her neck.

Only at the last moment, Kate realized what was going on and bent over backward to avoid being decapitated.

Crux didn't stop, but reversed the movement of his double-edged sword and now attempted to slice her torso in half.

This attack was also just barely blocked by Kate's left katana.

He was fast!

This guy is incredible, she thought , taking a quick step back. *Not sure I am better with swords than he is. Time to take it to the next level.* She reached for the belt and pressed the booster injection button three times in a row.

Her doctor told her a while ago that each injection may shorten her life by, perhaps, a month or so. This didn't worry Kate yet—like most young people, she wasn't yet thinking much about dying at an old age.

"What did you mean when you said you are not truly alive?" Kate asked, trying to buy a few seconds before the booster kicked in.

"I am not going to tell you anything anymore," Crux responded. "Join us and you will find out."

"Let's talk about it later," Kate replied and suddenly accelerated towards Crux. She went straight at him, but changed her direction at the last moment and moved to her right, around him. She moved so fast he barely reacted to her first move and missed the second. She swung her katana and cut deep into his left bicep. Blood squirted in all directions and Crux stepped back, holding his sword with one hand only.

Kate had a difficult time controlling herself now as she felt the urge to keep cutting and stabbing the enemy until he was dead. But, she forced herself to stop and wait for his next action.

She wanted him alive.

"I see," Crux said in a calm voice. "The typical human trickery. When you cannot beat someone fair and square, you change the rules or you cheat."

"Drop the sword," Kate said in a trembling voice. "We have a lot to talk about. Don't make me finish you."

"We will talk later when I see you again," he responded.

Suddenly, he grimaced, made a screeching sound, grimaced again as if in pain, and collapsed on his back next to his dead partner.

"Wait!" Kate jumped forward and leaned over Crux's body, but he was already dead, foam coming from his mouth.

"Shit!" she yelled. "Shit! The bastard poisoned himself! How are we going to interrogate them now?"

"Maybe, we can hack their cyber-augmentations?" suggested Larsen, who'd quietly joined Kate next to the two bodies.

"I doubt they are that stupid," Kate replied. "Probably, he did the self-destruct thing as well and burned every circuit inside his stupid cyber-augment."

"Either way, what's done is done," Larsen concluded philosophically. "And the colonel wants to talk to you."

"Right now?"

"Yes, right now."

Feeling tired, disappointed, and frustrated with what she considered a failure, Kate waited for a few more minutes for the booster effect to fade and walked downstairs to talk to the old man.

❀ ❀ ❀

"What happened up there?" Clarkson asked and stared at Kate, giving her a chance to formulate a reply.

"It is hard to explain, sir," she said. "You were right— something is fishy. There is something very weird about these two and their boss."

"Boss?"

"Ah, you didn't receive any transmissions? I will make the recordings available to you later. These two are a part of some elaborate plan. Some kind of next evolutionary movement... a revolution of some sort, or something like that. I even spoke with their boss!"

"Really?" The colonel was clearly interested.

"Yes, sir. He offered me to join them. He said something about our imperfections and him offering the ultimate solution—"

"Sounds like ordinary crazy talk to me."

"Yes... No, it didn't feel like this to me. It didn't feel stupid, at least. Crazy, perhaps. But also, pretty smart. It felt real somehow."

"So, both suspects are dead?" Colonel changed the subject. "We will never find out what this was all about?"

"Hmm... they promised to find me. The boss said this was just the beginning, the first wave."

"And you believe him?"

"Yes. Somehow, I do."

"Are you worried about it?"

"Hmm... I am not afraid if that is what you mean. I do worry, however, because I felt this is something bigger than what we suspected. Way beyond these two weird guys. With, perhaps, many more people being involved."

"Hmm... what do you think his main message was for you? It seems like it made quite an impression?"

"Well, he made me realize what I already knew... We live in a very confusing time, sir. Humans, transhumans, connected humans, androids, embedded AI... it all looks exciting but there is something wrong about it. The entire construct is unstable. 'Something is rotten in the state of Denmark,' as someone once said. And it cannot continue like this forever. Eventually, one side, one solution will prevail. And I am not sure which one. And this makes me worried."

Colonel, who was listening to Kate attentively, coughed into his fist and remained silent for close to a minute.

"Have you learned anything that can help us locate that mysterious 'Master' you spoke with?" the colonel asked eventually.

"Nothing specific, sir." Kate hesitated before answering. "He mentioned waiting for half a century in some 'wet and humid jungle'... I am not sure what this means. And, there were some strange image flashes at the very end... just when he disconnected. Some mix of green leaves, trees, and a dark animal shape looking like... a rhinoceros, I think. Very strange and made no sense to me."

"Okay, then," the colonel exhaled and looked around. The Hunters were still moving near the building, loading dead and injured bodies into cars next to the entrance, cleaning up the mess they'd created during this short but violent encounter. "Go home, Kate, get some good rest. You did well today, thank you. And take this day off. On Monday, we'll start an investigation into this case. And you will lead it."

Kate wanted to ask for more details but just nodded to Colonel, turned around silently and went to look for her *Kamikaze Super X*, which was parked nearby. Five minutes later, she was back on the freeway, which was empty now, going in a direction away from the downtown at 100 mph.

Going home.

The city behind her had quieted down and finally fallen asleep, gathering all the needed energy for the coming day.

The night was finally upon it.

"You don't have to burn books to destroy a culture. Just get people to stop reading them."— Ray Bradbury

About the Author

Andre K. George has a Ph.D. in Engineering and has worked in the high-tech industry for over twenty years building and managing research and development organizations specializing in big data analytics, artificial intelligence, and the Internet of Things.

Science Fiction has been Andre's passion since he was a child, yet books to his liking in this genre are rare. However, as C.S. Lewis once said, "You can make anything by writing." And, at some point in his life, Andre asked himself, "Why not create the world I like and the characters I actually enjoy instead of waiting for the others to do it for me?"

That is how this book was born. The title of it is an homage to the famous novel by Isaac Asimov. If you are reading this book, you already know that.

Next Book Announcement:

Inteland

When the famous and outspoken professor Jack Backstrom is invited to the secretive Inteland lab in the Brazilian jungle to assist after an accident, he discovers that they are years ahead of the rest of the world when it comes to the development of Artificial Intelligence. Along with May, a powerful and highly-advanced AI living inside a supercomputer, Jack encounters a friendly, human-like Möbius and nine other robots.

But alongside these revolutionary advances, there is a darker side to Inteland's work. Hiding in the jungle's depths is Freaking Rhino, a mechanical beast that destroys his opponents at will and grows stronger and smarter with each passing victory by incorporating the victims' parts and software into itself.

Now, Freaking Rhino is set to be unleashed on an unsuspecting world and only Jack, the lab's founder Francis Olds, and his daughter and robotics engineer Keira, along with a small group of scientists and their AI allies, stand in its way.

Inteland will become available on **Amazon in November 2021.**

Made in the USA
Las Vegas, NV
15 January 2022

41443550R00096